AMULET BOOKS ★ NEW YORK

LISA GREENWALD

Dog Beach Unleashed

The Library of Congress has catalogued the hardcover edition of this book as follows:

Greenwald, Lisa.
Dog Beach unleashed / Lisa Greenwald
pages cm. — (The Seagate summers ; book 2)
Summary: Seagate Island's centennial summer should be a huge celebration of beach traditions, but it is the rainiest summer on record and Remy, Micayla, Bennett, and the C Twins find that tempers are short, dogs are bored, and summer magic is hard to find.
ISBN 9781419714818 (hardback) — ISBN 978-1-61312-765-0 (ebook)
[1. Summer—Fiction. 2. Vacations—Fiction. 3. Beaches—Fiction. 4. Friendship—Fiction. 5. Dogs—Fiction. 6. Dog walking—Fiction.] I. Title.
PZ7.G85199 Dog 2015
[Fic]—dc23
2014045255

ISBN for this edition: 978-1-4197-2056-7

ABRAMS
THE ART OF BOOKS SINCE 1949
115 West 18th Street
New York, NY 10011
www.abramsbooks.com

For Maggie Lehrman,
superstar editor

This is it. This moment. My favorite moment of the entire year.

I'm sitting in one of the movie-theater-like seats on the ferry. On the top level, of course. I watch the mainland disappear behind me, and then all I see is ocean. Ocean and ocean and ocean. And it feels like forever until I'll get there. *Hurry up*, I think. But then I change my mind. Don't hurry up. Let me enjoy this. Enjoy the almost there.

But then, little by little, I start to see it—bits and pieces of Seagate Island. I see the lighthouse and then the bright orange cottage that sits right on the shoreline. And I get closer. Closer and closer. And I see more things take shape.

My heart is flopping with excitement, like a caught fish that's about to get back into the water.

My mom is on one side of me, my dad on the other. Marilyn Monroe is on my lap. The whole summer is spread out in front of me like a big picnic blanket on the sand.

And this summer isn't like any other summer. This is Seagate's centennial summer. One hundred years since the first person came to Seagate. One hundred years of pink sunsets and Sundae Best's overflowing ice cream cups. One hundred years of flip-flops click-clacking on the boardwalk. One hundred years of Ping-Pong tournaments and summertime friends—some of the best friends in the world.

There's going to be a huge party—Seagate Island's birthday party—for everyone to celebrate together. Carnival rides. A photo booth. A talent show. Mrs. Pursuit volunteered to be in charge of the celebration committee. They've been planning it since last summer.

"I just got a text from Vivian." My mom taps my knee. "They took the earlier ferry."

I nod. "Oh. Okay."

Vivian Newhouse is Bennett's mom and one of my mom's best friends. They've known each other since Bennett and I were newborn babies. That's when Bennett and I met, too, although, obviously, I can't remember that meeting. He's one of those people who's always been there. There's never been a time when I didn't know Bennett Newhouse.

Bennett had texted me that they were taking the noon ferry, just like us. I looked for him everywhere but couldn't find him. Now I know why.

I wonder if Bennett will be waiting when we get there,

standing at the ferry terminal, looking for us as we come off the boat.

I haven't seen him in a whole year, and when I think about him, all I can picture is what he looked like at the end of last summer—shaggy hair, cargo shorts with holes in them, pizza-stained T-shirts. I'm sure he's gotten taller. Maybe he'll even be wearing new summer clothes. They won't be torn or stained. They'll look crisp, the tags just cut off. Everything fresh for a new summer.

I thought about Bennett this whole year. We e-mailed a lot and talked on the phone. But none of that's the same as being with him in person.

I flip-flopped back and forth all year long. Did I like him as more than a friend? Sometimes I thought I did. And sometimes I thought I didn't. I kept telling myself that I'd figure it out on Seagate. Things always seem clearer there. Everything makes more sense when you're near the ocean.

But there's one conversation we had that lingers in the back of my mind.

We were on the phone one Saturday night. It was February, the month when the past summer feels like a million years ago, and the next summer feels like a million years away.

It was after ten at night, and I'm never supposed to be on the phone that late. But my parents were out, and I'd told the babysitter I was going to bed. Which I was. But then Bennett called. And we were talking. Mostly about stupid stuff, like this crazy new burrito he'd tried, and the fact that people camp outside certain stores so they can be the first ones to get the new sneakers. But then he brought up first kisses. Something about this girl Mara who keeps a list of who in the grade has kissed someone and who hasn't.

"You haven't kissed anyone yet, right?" he asked me.

I stayed quiet, but then I said that no, I hadn't.

And he said he hadn't, either.

"Oh," I said.

"We could be each other's first kiss," he said, as if it were no big deal. As if he were saying we could play Ping-Pong or we could share a chocolate croissant or we could sit on his dock and throw pebbles into the ocean.

My heart thumped in my chest. And I said, "Sure."

But even as I was saying it, I was thinking that I wasn't sure I wanted that to happen. I told myself that even if it did happen, summer was so far away that I didn't need to worry about it or even think about it.

It was something I could deal with later.

I pushed the thought away. As far away as possible.

But that later is now quickly approaching. That far away is getting so much closer.

We'll be together for a whole summer. And I know I said *sure,* but now I don't know if I want to.

I look out the ferry window. We're almost there.

I keep thinking the same thing: Will I see him as Bennett, the same old Bennett I've always known? Or will I see him as something more? The way I saw him at the end of last summer.

A whole year has passed. Are we different now?

As much as I don't want to be different, I think I am. As much as I want everything to always stay the same, I know that things change. And I know that change can be okay, that I can handle it. *Sometimes*, anyway.

But the one thing I can't handle is the not knowing. I always want to know how things are going to work out.

When I start a book, I skip ahead and read the last page first. Always. I don't read mysteries. I hate surprise parties.

Marilyn Monroe smiles her gentle Yorkie smile. She looks up at me and licks my chin, as if she senses I can use some reassuring. I wonder if she knows where we're going. I've told her a million times. I even showed her the countdown calendar I had on my computer and the real, paper calendar I had hanging above my desk, with all the days that had been X-ed off in red marker.

"We're almost there, Mari," I whisper. Her ears perk up, and she shuffles on my lap. "Sit, sit. A little while longer."

"So, all your clients know you're coming back?" my dad asks me. "Do you need to have an orientation for the dogs? Get them ready for camp or anything?"

I smile. "That's a good idea, actually. Maybe we should have some kind of easing-in process, like I had for preschool and kindergarten?"

Everyone needs time to get situated, to warm up. Even

dogs. Life is like a freezing-cold pool that way. We all need to dip a toe before we jump in.

"Good thinking, Rem." My mom pats my leg, and I wonder if she's as excited as I am. She's been coming to Seagate Island for over forty years now, since her own childhood. I wonder if this amazing anticipation ever fades. After year twenty do you start to get used to it?

I want to ask her, but what if the answer's yes? That it's not as exciting as it used to be? If it is, I don't want to know.

"Remmmmyyyyyyy," I hear someone yell as soon as we're off the boat, and even though it's lovely to be welcomed this way, the greeting is not from the person I hoped to see first.

"Hi, Mason." I smile. "How was your year?"

"Excellent. And yours?"

"Great." I look around. Is Bennett here? Micayla? Mason Redmond, Micayla's crush, can't be here to greet *me*. He must be looking for someone else. He's nice and everything, but we're not "wait at the ferry" kind of friends.

He reads my mind. "Micayla went into the pharmacy to get some more sunscreen. She told me to wait for you and let you know that she'd be right out." He clips the sunglasses attachment onto his glasses. "Anyway, ciao. I'm going to be late for my Italian class."

Italian class? School just ended; Mason's probably only been on Seagate for a day or two. And he's already studying something.

I stand there, holding Marilyn Monroe in my arms, and watch Mason walk away. I'm searching for Bennett out of the corner of my eye when I feel an arm around my neck and smell the familiar scent of strawberry shampoo.

"Micayla!" I turn around and throw one arm over her shoulders, and we hug and sway with Marilyn Monroe sandwiched between us.

"You're here! You're here! You're here!" She pulls back from the hug finally, and puts her hands on her hips, inspecting me. "And you look so fabulous! You cut your hair? And you didn't even tell me!"

"It was just a trim," I explain.

"No," she insists. "Way more than a trim. It's above your shoulders now! And it already looks lighter from the sun. It's only June!"

"You look amazing," I say. "Your braids are perfect! Did you just get them done?"

"Uh-huh!"

We go back and forth about our hair, and then a beach ball hits me in the head. I turn to look around to see where it came from.

"Sorry! I wanted to get your attention, but I guess that wasn't the best method."

It's Bennett. *My* Bennett. He's right here in front of me.

Royal-blue mesh shorts and a faded gray T-shirt. A buzz cut with a tiny piece sticking up on the top of his head. His shaggy hair is gone.

"Yeah, not the best method" is all I manage to say. The only thing I can think about is how different he looks. How much taller he's gotten. How he's already tan and he's only been here for an hour.

"Remy," he groans. "Don't be so serious. Get out of your New York City mind-set and into your Seagate one. Now!" He yells the last part in a joking way and hits me on the arm, all playful-like.

I smile. "Done and done."

"Well, go settle in, Rem," Micayla tells me. "Meet us at the stadium when you're done. Bennett just organized a 'Welcome Back Ping-Pong Tournament' for all the kids whose parents are busy unpacking."

"Genius idea," I tell them. "Be there soon."

Bennett and Micayla walk in the other direction, and Marilyn Monroe and I stroll to my house. I've been here less than an hour and l already feel great. There's something about the Seagate Island air. As soon as it touches your skin, you're rejuvenated.

Marilyn Monroe and I walk slowly, taking in all the Seagate sights, saying hi to people we know, and stopping to pee a few times. (Mari—not me.)

I keep wondering how it was possible for Bennett to look so different, so much older, today. I guess a lot can change in a year. But why wasn't he waiting for me at the ferry? I guess he was there soon after. Maybe he was too busy setting up that Ping-Pong tournament? Maybe he was as nervous to see me as I was to see him.

I wish life was a movie right now. I want to fast-forward to the end, just for a quick second, to see how it unfolds. And then I'll rewind back to right now so I can go through the whole thing and enjoy it.

With all the technology in the world, it's disappointing that there's still no way to see the future.

The whole summer is ahead of us, and I can't help but wonder what's going to happen.

I wake up with a jolt. It's always like this my first morning on Seagate. At first I think I'm in my New York City apartment, and then I look around. I hear the quiet, and I smell the ocean air wafting through my open window.

And then I know. I stay in bed, breathe it in, and appreciate the perfection that is the first Seagate morning.

"Remy." Mom knocks on my door and then comes in. "Dad and I are going for a walk on the beach. Want to come?"

"I want to stay in bed a little while longer," I answer. "I'll see you when you get back."

"Sounds good. MM has already been out and fed."

"Thanks, Mom." Even though Marilyn Monroe is really my dog, my parents help out and take care of her, too. They won't admit it, but I know they love having a dog in the house again. They practically fight over who gets to walk her in the morning, since they're both such early risers.

It's hard to believe that Marilyn Monroe's original owner, Amber Seasons, isn't here this summer. She's a Seagate lifer, but her husband got transferred to work in Australia for a few years, so that's where they are now. She finds time to video chat with Marilyn Monroe at least once a week. Mari still remembers her and gets so excited every time she sees Amber on the screen.

I roll over and check my phone. I have a text from Micayla, a text from Bennett, and a text from Claire. Micayla and Bennett are going to Mornings for croissants, and Claire's already at the community pool, working on her tan.

I don't know who to text back first or where I should go. Any girl would want this problem, but it still stresses me out a little bit. Bennett and Micayla don't really know that Claire and I got pretty close over the school year. She lives in Westchester, but both her parents work in Manhattan, so she comes in pretty often. She even slept over a few times. I shouldn't feel guilty about this, but I do. At the end of last summer, we were all friends, but it was still kind of an unspoken thing that Claire was more of a side friend, not part of the core group.

While I'm changing into my bathing suit and trying to cream cheese a bagel at the same time, my phone rings. It's Claire.

"Bring a towel," she says. "They haven't upgraded since

last summer. They're still using the tiny washcloth ones, and they're super scratchy."

"Will do."

"Are you coming?" she whines.

"Yup. Leaving in five. Just finishing a bagel."

"Ooh. Bring me one?"

I tell her okay, and I pack my beach bag with a towel, snacks, a water bottle, sunscreen, a hat, and everything else I'll need for the day. I refill Marilyn Monroe's water bowl and leave a note telling my parents where I'm going.

Marilyn Monroe looks at me with sad eyes and makes me feel guilty for leaving her behind.

"We'll go to Daisy's later," I tell her. "I promise." Daisy McDougal owns a restaurant on Seagate, but unlike grumpy Beverly at Mornings, she loves dogs and always gives them treats.

Mari lets out a resigned whimper and hops up onto the couch by the bay window.

I walk over to the community pool wearing my brand-new paisley cover-up with my polka-dot one-piece. My silver flip-flops *clop-clop* against the sidewalk, already giving me a blister. I try to ignore it.

Micayla runs up behind me and taps my shoulder. "Where are you going?"

"Oh, um, to the pool to meet Claire. How was Mornings?"

"Delish, but Beverly is even grumpier than last summer. It's a little hard to believe."

I scowl. "What was she like during the year?"

"She wasn't here much," Micayla tells me. "She hired some people to run the place during the winter."

"Oh." I shrug. Since Micayla lives on Seagate all year now, I keep waiting for her to tell me some juicy year-rounder secrets, but so far she hasn't shared anything all that exciting. I also expect her to tell me she can't hang out because she needs to spend time with her year-rounder friends, but she hasn't done that, either. "Come with me to the pool," I tell her.

"Sure. I already have my suit on." She grabs my hand, and we walk to the pool talking about who was at Mornings and who we're excited to see.

"I didn't even know Claire was here already," Micayla says. "I haven't seen her. When did she arrive?"

"Yesterday, maybe? Two days ago?" I actually do know the answer—she and her brother, Calvin, came to their grandfather Mr. Brookfield's house on Seagate three days ago because their mom had to go to a conference and their dad is traveling in Europe. But for some reason, I don't tell Micayla that. I don't want her to feel left out. Also, I'm not sure I should tell her what's been going on with Claire and Calvin's parents. It looks like they're going to get a divorce, and divorce seems like such a private thing. Definitely not something to gossip about. Claire will tell Micayla when she's ready.

"So, when are we starting up doggie day care?" Micayla

asks, throwing her arm over my shoulders. "You have no idea how many people asked me about it during the year. It was like they expected me to keep it going, even without you. Like I would ever do that."

"You could have." I look at her and raise my eyebrows. "You're fully capable."

"Thanks, Rem. But no. It's your thing. Anyway, we should get it started soon. People are eager for their dogs to do some socializing."

I laugh. "Really?"

"Oh yeah. Mr. Jennings even said that Atticus is getting bored with only Rascal to play with." Paul Jennings is a Seagate local who also happens to be Micayla's teacher, and his German shepherd hangs out a lot with the Newfoundland who belongs to the mom of Paul's girlfriend, Andi.

I'm glad to hear it. We made a lot of money last summer, and I'm hoping to make even more this year. I want to be able to donate all of it to an animal shelter in Manhattan that's in danger of closing.

We get to the pool and find Claire in the direct sun on one of the sea-green lounge chairs. A thick brown towel is underneath her. Her skin is frying. She thinks that tanning oil with SPF 4 is as good as sunscreen.

"Girlies!" Claire yelps and sits up. She ties her hair into a high bun and dries the sweat off her forehead with a corner of her towel. "I'd hug you, but I'm really sweaty. Like, really, really sweaty."

"We can see that." I laugh. "Air hug!"

Micayla and I pretend to put our arms around her. Then we spread our towels out on lounges and lie down.

"Do I look tan yet?" Claire asks us. "I think I'm the palest person on this whole island."

"Give it time," Micayla says. "It's still June." Since she has perfect dark skin naturally, Micayla never understands Claire's obsession with tanning.

Claire turns onto her side to face me. "So, what ever happened with that girl at your school who tried out for that movie and was sure she was gonna get the part?"

"Oh yeah. She didn't get it. But she got a part in some other movie, so she's leaving school and getting tutored on the set."

"What on earth are you guys talking about?" Micayla asks.

"When I slept over at Remy's a few weeks ago, this girl Dylan called to tell her she was going to be in a movie with Brad Pitt, and she was leaving school and all this stuff. But then I never found out if she really got the part," Claire explains.

It's really not the most exciting story in the world, but Claire thought it was so cool. I was supposed to keep her updated, but I forgot all about it.

Micayla glares at me, and I know what her eyes are saying. "I didn't know you slept over at Remy's," she says to Claire.

"Oh yeah, a bunch of times." Claire smiles. "What, like, ten maybe? Right, Rem?"

My chest flames like the sunburn blossoming on Claire's forehead. I should have told Micayla about the sleepovers. I didn't purposely *not* tell her, but I guess I didn't go out of my way to tell her, either.

I nod and attempt to change the subject. "Anyway, you guys, we need to discuss doggie day care. Mic tells me that people are eager to get their pooches settled into the routine. And I'm eager to raise money for the shelter."

I look at Claire and then at Micayla, and I still sense the confusion and sadness Micayla is feeling. I'll talk to her about it later. I'll make it right. I mean, she was on Seagate. It's not as if she could come to Manhattan just for a plain old sleepover.

"Well, we can't discuss this without Bennett," Micayla says. "That wouldn't be right. So how about we have a meeting on the beach later? Or during lunch?"

"A lunch meeting sounds great," I say. "Pastrami on Rye around noon? I'll text Bennett."

"Sounds good to me," Claire says. "Should we text Calvin, or is he with Bennett?"

"Text him," Micayla says. "I don't want anyone to feel *left out*."

Maybe she doesn't really mean anything by that comment, but it still stings. I need to smooth things over soon, because we can't start the summer like this. It won't be good for the dogs. Or for us.

Claire and Micayla stop at SGI Sweets for some sour straws on the way to Pastrami on Rye. I want them to have a few minutes to bond without me, so I stay outside on the bench to soak up the sun.

"Hi, Remy." Mr. Aprone, the owner of Novel Ideas, Seagate's bookstore, stops to talk to me. I haven't seen him yet, and I'm excited to discuss the plans for the Centennial Summer celebration with him.

"How was your year?" I ask him.

"Good, good." He snaps open his water bottle and takes a sip. "But please bring the gang by, okay? I'm worried it's going to be a short summer, and I need as much business as I can get. You know how it is, with so many e-readers these days."

I nod. He's always working so hard to make sure people

still read books on paper. I totally understand. I love books on paper, too.

"What do you mean, a short summer?" I ask.

He sits down next to me. "You haven't heard?"

I shake my head and turn around to look in the window of SGI Sweets. Claire and Micayla are taking forever in there.

"It's going to be a rough hurricane season. Everyone's saying it could be one of the worst we've ever seen. There's a good chance a dangerous storm could reach Seagate."

"Really?" I wish he hadn't told me that. Could it be some kind of joke? I highly doubt anyone would find it funny.

"Sadly, yes." He raises his eyebrows. "Listen, I need to run. But it's good to see you, Remy. Stop by the store, okay? I have the newest title in that series you love."

"Thanks. I'll come in soon, and we can talk about the Centennial celebration, too."

Claire and Micayla come out of SGI Sweets, and I don't mention the dangerous storm Mr. Aprone was worried about. We walk, and I try to pretend he didn't just tell me that bit of news. I push it out of my brain, refusing to believe it. Just because someone predicts a hurricane doesn't mean it's going to happen.

A short summer would be disastrous. It's already short enough. I need all the time I can get on Seagate.

We walk into Pastrami on Rye, and Bennett and Calvin are waiting for us in the back booth. They're spitting bits of wadded-up paper at each other through straws, cracking up.

When Calvin sees us, he stops immediately. He sits up straighter, as if he's suddenly serious and grown-up. It's kind of funny to watch, but it makes me happy. We all have a business to run, so I want our customers to know that we're responsible and mature.

"What's shakin'?" he asks as we sit down. "We ordered our burgers already. I got the Hurricane Hammie. Obviously."

I wish the owners would take that off the menu. After what Mr. Aprone said, we should abolish the word *hurricane* from the Seagate Island vocabulary, even when it's only referring to hamburgers.

"First of all, gross. There's no reason to have a fried egg on a hamburger. And second of all, you guys couldn't wait for us to get here?" Claire asks. "Sheesh. Didn't you just eat breakfast, like, two hours ago?"

"We're hungry," Bennett explains.

"Obviously," Claire mutters.

The waitress comes over and brings us menus. We order two of their famous oversized deli sandwiches, a basket of fries, and a basket of onion rings to share.

"Okay, so let's get down to business," I say to get the ball rolling. "I've already run into a few of our old clients, and the owners are itching to get the dogs back on a schedule."

I need to pretend that everything is fine. Get the doggie

day care business started and keep the critters happy. If I act as if this is a normal summer, maybe it will be.

"Well, we should make room for new clients, too," Bennett suggests. "We should advertise and see how many dogs we can take on. Claire and Calvin are officially on board this summer, right, guys?"

They nod.

"So we have two extra sets of hands," Bennett continues. "We can really expand the business."

"But do we want to be so busy?" Micayla asks after a bite of sandwich. "We need to save some time for fun, too, right?"

"Yes. Definitely. Fun and tanning," Claire answers.

We agree and decide to make some posters so that everyone on Seagate is aware of our business. We'll follow up with our regular clients, and we'll get everything going by next week.

"So we have the rest of this week just to hang out and have fun," I explain.

"Thanks for the permission, Rem," Bennett says, mocking me.

Bennett has always been the kind of friend who teases, who helps me break out of my usually serious frame of mind. But right now it's annoying. I don't know why. I just want him to be serious for once. Like Calvin.

We spend the next morning hanging out and putting up posters about our doggie day care business, but when afternoon rolls around, our group is off in a million different directions. Micayla goes to a yoga class with her mom. Calvin and Claire go on some mystery adventure with Mr. Brookfield, their grandpa.

Bennett and I are left alone with a whole afternoon in front of us.

For some reason it makes my stomach feel queasy.

"What are you doing now?" he asks when it's just us.

"No idea. You?"

"Well, I haven't been in your new pool yet this summer. So let's do that." He looks at me, but I can't look back at him. Bennett and me alone at my pool? It was never a big deal before. But now it makes me nervous.

"Sound okay?" he asks.

I realize I haven't answered him.

"Oh yeah. Sounds great."

We get to my house, and I tell him that I need to run up to my room to change. Truth is, I already have my bathing suit on. But I need to mentally prepare.

"Go out to the pool. I'll meet you there," I tell him.

I don't want to feel different. I want it to be Bennett and me swimming together as we have a million times on Seagate. But as much as I tell myself that nothing's changed, something has.

Suddenly Bennett seeing me in my swimsuit is the scariest thing in the world. I want to swim in one of my dad's oversized T-shirts instead.

When I get to the pool, Bennett is sprawled out on a lounge chair reading a section of my dad's newspaper.

"Do you have any idea what's going on with the real estate market in New York?" he asks. "It's totally insane. You guys should sell your apartment. You would make so much money."

"Um, okay." I give him a look. "I don't really pay attention to real estate. And I didn't think you did, either."

He laughs. "Well, I don't, I guess. I was just reading this article. But don't I sound smart?"

"You do, Bennett. Very smart."

We both crack up, and he puts the newspaper on the little

side table. He takes off his SGI Sweets T-shirt, throws it at me, and says, "Ready to swim?"

I don't want his smelly T-shirt on me, so I throw it back at him.

I should've gotten into the pool while he was still reading the paper. Then he couldn't watch me walk all the way from the lounges to the pool ladder. But it's too late for all that now.

Thankfully, he takes a running leap into the pool, and I have just enough time to get down the ladder and into the water before he comes up for air.

"Your new pool is awesome! And it's the perfect temperature," he says.

I can't think of a single thing to say, and I have no idea why. Bennett's been my best summertime friend forever, but my mind is blank.

"Get on the pink raft," he says. "I'll push you around the pool. Remember how we always used to do that when we were little?"

I sneer. "Yeah, but have you gotten any better at it? You tipped me over a few too many times for me to trust you and your raft-driving skills."

"I've been practicing." He flicks some pool water at me and smiles. "Come on. Don't be scared. Get on the raft."

I don't know how to get out of it. Now he's going to see me—my whole body—lying flat on the raft.

Bennett holds the raft still for me, and luckily I'm able to get up on the first try. Usually I fumble around and half fall off in the most clumsy, ungraceful way possible.

But today I'm able to do it. I'm grateful for that.

My head rests on the little raft pillow, and I let out a sigh of relief. I cover my stomach with my arms, and Bennett pushes me around the pool.

"So, what happens next year? Where are you going to school?"

I tell him about the whole middle school process in New York City—how you have to apply to some schools to get in. It's pretty complicated, almost like applying to college.

"Your friends are going to that same school?" he asks.

"Well, some are, and some aren't."

We get so involved in a conversation about school and standardized tests and all that boring stuff that I forget I'm floating on a raft in my swimsuit with Bennett pushing me around. And I forget that he likes to flip me over when I'm not paying attention.

And that's exactly what happens.

He flips over the pink raft, and I fly off into the water. I come up for air, coughing and laughing and splashing Bennett as much as I can.

And then Bennett and I are standing so close to each other in the pool that we're practically touching. Suddenly I get freaked out all over again.

"So, what should we do now?" he asks.

I'm relieved that Bennett has changed the mood.

"Do you have any good snacks? I'm starving," he adds.

"Hmm. Well, we did just get here and go grocery shopping. So we should be at our snack peak of the summer, shouldn't we?"

"Good point. Let's go raid the fridge!"

"Go on inside," I tell him. "I want to swim a lap first."

This is a total lie, but I don't want to get out of the water with him watching me.

"You're suddenly into exercise?" he asks me.

"Well, I'm trying," I explain, hoping I sound believable. "I might even try out for my school's swim team this year."

"Wow. Impressive." He arches an eyebrow. And there's a reason for him to be surprised. I've never been into sports. When I say I like to swim, I mean that I like to wade in the water and float around.

"Hey, I have an idea. I could be your coach this summer!" he says. "Get you ready for tryouts."

As soon as he says it, I realize my mistake. Bennett is an amazing swimmer. He took lessons from the time he was six months old. If he's my coach, he's going to see me in a bathing suit all the time. I mean, he would anyway, since we swim every day on Seagate. But this would be different. This would be up close and personal.

"You don't seem enthused by the idea," he says.

"I guess I'm realizing all the time and effort it would take, and I got tired just thinking about it." I laugh. "You know me. I don't like to exert too much energy."

"Right. But I do want to make use of this great new pool." He shrugs. "Well, it's just an idea. And it would be fun to hang out more."

He wraps a yellow towel around his shoulders and goes into the house.

I stay in the pool and think about this coaching idea, and part of it seems enticing—all that alone time with Bennett. But it makes me nervous, too.

I wish I understood what I was feeling.

The next day, we hit the ground running, trying to get the business going again. The boys put up posters on the parts of the island that we've missed, and the girls follow up with all our old clients, making sure we know what their needs are so we can give them priority in the schedule.

"We're going to be very busy this summer," Paul, Atticus's dog-dad, tells us.

Micayla, Claire, and I are sitting with Paul and his girl-friend, Andi, on his porch. Atticus and Rascal are gnawing on rawhide chews in a corner. Atticus's triangular German shepherd ears perk up and he tries to steal Rascal's rawhide. They behave like real brothers now that they live together, always wrestling and snatching each other's treats. But Rascal stays calm. His black, velvety Newfoundland fur almost glistens in the sun. He sits there all dignified, as if he doesn't have a care in the world.

"We are?" Andi asks Paul with stars in her eyes. They share the wicker love seat, sitting as close to each other as they possibly can.

He nods. "Yup. I have a lot of things planned."

Maybe he knows about the shortened summer, too. Maybe he's trying to squeeze in as much as he can before the big storm. Ever since I talked to Mr. Aprone, I've been worrying about it, but I keep the worries to myself.

Right now it feels like a secret that only Mr. Aprone and I know. If I don't talk about it, maybe it won't become real.

Paul grabs Andi's hand, and I wonder if Claire and Micayla feel as awkward as I do. It seems as if we caught the grown-up couple in some intimate moment, even though they knew we were coming over.

"Which reminds me," Paul continues. "I wanted to ask you if you ever take dogs overnight."

The three of us look at one another.

"How on earth would they do that, Paul?" Andi yelps. "They're kids, not a kennel!"

He shrugs. "Just thought I'd ask. No need to bite my head off!"

She kisses him on the forehead. "Sorry."

"Well, no one has ever asked us that," I reply. I don't know exactly how we'd do it. But I hate to say no. I guess we could always beg our parents to let us keep the dogs in our houses.

"Well, keep it in mind," Paul says. "Andi's mom could use some extra help with Rascal."

Micayla's been pretty much silent this whole time, looking at her feet and fiddling with the strings on her hoodie. And then I realize she probably feels weird sitting on her teacher's porch, watching him hold hands with his girlfriend.

"Can you watch both dogs every morning until about two or three in the afternoon?" Andi says. "If you want to pick them up, that would be great, but we like to go for a morning stroll, so we can always drop them at Dog Beach, too."

I write that all down and then look up. "Picking them up works." I turn to face Micayla and Claire. "You guys cool with that?"

They nod.

"Okay, so we should be up and running by early next week, I think," I tell them. "We just need to iron out the schedule with our other clients, and then we'll be ready to go. Anything new we should know about?"

Andi and Paul look at each other and laugh a little bit. "Nothing, really," Andi says. "The dogs are happy as clams, and they love being together."

"Just like us," Paul says.

"Sounds great," I reply, and I stand up.

"Really great," Claire adds, as if it's something she feels she's supposed to say but not necessarily something she feels.

Micayla looks down at her feet again. "See you guys soon," she says. "We're excited about taking care of Atticus and Rascal again."

Claire needs to go home, so Micayla and I decide to walk to Mornings to get a snack. I'm happy to have some alone time with her. I hope she's not still feeling left out.

"That was weird, wasn't it?" I ask her. "Was it crazy to be at your teacher's place?"

"Yeah, I couldn't wait to leave. And Mr. Jennings was just being so strange. Wasn't he? What kind of plans do you think he was talking about?"

"Maybe getting married?" I shrug. "Who knows?" I pull up the hood on my windbreaker as the breeze kicks up and it starts to rain.

Finally we're at Mornings, and thankfully grumpy Beverly isn't there.

We take a table by the window and share a chocolate croissant, an apple cinnamon muffin, and two hot chocolates. It's cold and gray and rainy. Not a good way to start the summer.

I look outside, and everything seems ominous. Maybe Mr. Aprone was right and a dangerous storm is going to swamp Seagate Island this summer.

"What are we gonna do with the dogs if it rains like this all the time?" I ask Micayla. Maybe she knows something about a ferocious hurricane season and isn't telling me.

"I was just thinking the same thing," Micayla answers. "I

don't know. We were so lucky last summer. Only a little drizzle here and there. No real rainy days."

"Think Mr. Brookfield would let us bring all the dogs to his basement?" I ask. "There's not much down there. Just boxes of random stuff."

"I don't think that would be great for the dogs," Micayla says. "It's not really that big. They wouldn't be able to run around."

I guess she's right.

"Bennett is a giant now, isn't he?" Micayla asks me, totally changing the subject.

"A giant?" I cover my mouth and giggle. I'm picturing Bennett as the Jolly Green Giant, and I can't stop laughing.

"He's taller than he was last summer!" she says defensively.

"He *is* taller," I admit.

We sit and talk and finish our treats, and Micayla fills me in about what happens on Seagate after everyone leaves.

"So you know those grills down by the stadium that anyone can use?" she asks.

I nod.

"Last October, everyone left on the island came out with stuff to grill, and we had this giant barbecue." She takes a sip of her hot chocolate. "It was crazy. The parents were totally living it up. They had music playing, and they were all dancing. It was really kind of weird to see the parents acting so silly, but it was kind of fun, too. They were like teenagers!

Anyway, I think that's when Daisy got into a fight with Mrs. Pursuit, and I'm pretty sure they haven't spoken since."

"What was the fight over?" I ask.

"I don't know. Something about the placement of garbage cans on Seagate. It got really heated." Micayla takes the last bite of muffin, and we clear our plates. "It's really sad. They've been best friends since they were our age."

"Listen, I'm sorry I didn't tell you that Claire slept over," I say. "It wasn't a big deal, but I should've told you. I'm sorry if you felt left out."

She nods and finishes her last sip of hot chocolate. "Feeling left out might be the worst feeling in the world."

"I know." I put my arm over Micayla's shoulders. "Promise me we'll never fight over something as dumb as garbage can placement?" I ask, and we start laughing.

"Of course not." Micayla puts her arm around my waist. "I promise."

Our posters are up all over the island, and business is booming.

Well, it's almost booming. We haven't actually spent time with any of the new dogs. Or even our former clients. We're just organizing the schedules for pickups and drop-offs and what hours they'll be at doggie day care. Because there's one problem: there's no place to take them. The usual sunny weather we have at Seagate has changed. Now it rains and rains and rains. I haven't even been in my pool since the day Bennett tipped over my raft, and Claire is miserable about her nonexistent tan.

"What am I going to do?" Claire asks.

Micayla, Claire, and I are at Mr. Brookfield's house, and we're watching one of his DVDs. He has the best collection of old scary movies and is the voice of a famous scream that was used in most of them. We fast-forward until we get to his scream parts.

"It'll stop raining," I assure her. "It never rains all summer long. It's unheard of."

"This is the palest I've ever been," Claire says. "Seriously. This summer is off to a bad start."

I keep telling her over and over again that it's going to be fine, but I know I'm just trying to convince myself. I can't control the weather. I can't control her tan. And more important, I don't know where we can take the dogs if they can't go to Dog Beach.

Lately, Claire's moods seem as erratic as the weather. One minute she's whining about her tan, but the next minute she looks as if she's going to cry. I can't blame her for being worried about her parents. It seems like one day out of the blue, they just stopped wanting to be married. Her dad said he wanted to move out. And that was that.

"I just don't get it," she says. "We were a family once. We really were." She looks at us, almost as if she expects us to have some kind of answer.

"You're still a family," I insist. "Really."

But as I say it, I wonder if it's true. Everything I say lately feels like a lie. Or not the whole truth.

Micayla stays quiet. She rubs Claire's back, and my stomach clenches with worry. Claire hates it when people get sentimental, and I'm afraid she'll lash out at Micayla when she's just trying to be kind.

But Claire doesn't say anything. She doesn't lash out. She just looks down at her feet and wipes away her tears with a shirtsleeve.

My stomach twists like a wrung-out washcloth. The combination of the rain and Claire's sadness is too much. I push the worried feelings away. The sun will come out, and Claire's parents will stay together. Everything will work out.

We finish the movie, and Mr. Brookfield makes us grilled cheese sandwiches and tomato soup for lunch. I'm enjoying our girls-only lunch, but it doesn't last very long. Soon Calvin and Bennett burst through the front door, dripping wet and covered in mud.

"Hi, ladies," Bennett says. "Mudsliding got a little crazy today."

For the most part, Seagate Island is pretty flat. But there's one hill on the other side of the island near the lighthouse, and it's pretty much only used for one thing: mudsliding.

"What happened?" I ask between bites of grilled cheese.

He sighs. "Well, it turns out the hill is a little rockier than usual. Calvin cut his face, so Mrs. Pursuit invited us into her house to get cleaned up. Then we got stuck there for a while sampling her new cookie recipes and looking through the photos she's trying to organize for the Centennial."

"That doesn't sound so bad," Micayla says.

"Yeah, the photos must be awesome," I jump in.

Bennett continues. "Well, yeah, that was okay, I guess, except for Calvin's cut face. Oh, and on the way home we ran into Lester and the Decsinis! They're back, and not just for a week this time, but the whole summer!"

"I'm going to change." Calvin barely looks at us. He doesn't say anything else and runs right upstairs. Maybe he's really hurt.

Bennett takes off his muddy shoes and rolls up his pants, then takes a seat on the floor next to me.

"So, how's Lester?" I ask, and I offer him a piece of my sandwich.

He grabs the sandwich as if he's starving. "He's still his adorable cocker spaniel self. But his owner-mom said he's gotten a little mischievous."

Bennett takes off his sweatshirt, and a little sliver of his stomach shows for a few seconds. I look away.

"Mischievous? That's interesting. Lester's smart," I say. "He always knew where we kept the extra treats."

Calvin joins the conversation as he comes down the stairs. I didn't even realize he was listening. "I love that dog," he says. He's holding an ice pack to his forehead, half of one eye covered with a bandage. "I think he was my favorite of all the dogs last summer."

Calvin sits down on the floor next to Bennett, and my first instinct is to go over and hug him. But that seems crazy. Me hugging *Calvin*. I don't know where this impulse is coming from. I look at him with his cut face, sitting there looking so sad. I wonder how he feels about the whole situation with his parents. He hasn't said much.

Later that day, Bennett and I walk home together. Micayla's mom picked her up at Mr. Brookfield's because they're going out for a family dinner at Frederick's Fish. Claire stayed quiet the rest of the afternoon, and I felt bad about it. She seems so sad.

I kept trying to think of things to say to her. Comforting things. Helpful things. But nothing came to me. I couldn't even say the sun was shining or tell her how great her tan was going to be.

"Are you okay?" Bennett asks as we're walking.

We've been quiet the whole time, which is unusual for us. My mind just keeps flopping back and forth between Claire's situation and being alone with Bennett—and the urge I had before to give Calvin a hug.

It's impossible to focus on making conversation when you have that much on your mind.

"Yeah. I'm fine." I look down at my Pumas. "Why?"

"You just seem quiet. I don't know. Like something's wrong."

"Nah. I'm fine." I don't feel like talking now. That's all I really know. But I don't feel like dealing with the silence, either. So I try to think of something to talk about. "Hey, maybe I will take you up on that swim-coach thing," I say. "If it ever stops raining, I mean."

I don't know why I say it. I'm not even sure I want to try out for the swim team. And I know I don't want to wear a bathing suit around Bennett every day. But sometimes when I can't think of what to say, I say the craziest thing possible.

Maybe Bennett could help me help Claire.

That sounds funny. Help me help someone else. But maybe that's what I need to do. Ask Bennett. He's helpful; he always has good advice. He's always so calm and relaxed. I need someone strong to lean on if I'm going to be able to help Claire.

"Really?" Bennett seems surprised, too.

"Yeah, I mean, you're on your school's swim team, and I want to get better, and, I don't know . . ." My voice trails off.

"Sure. Sounds great."

We get to my house and say good-bye, and Bennett tells me his mom is making fish kebabs for dinner if I want to come over.

"I'm gonna eat with my parents," I tell him. "Thanks anyway."

"Okay. See you tomorrow, Rem."

Over the course of the year, Bennett and I did this thing where we'd e-mail each other what we ate for dinner. It started because my dad made this really gross dinner he called Scramble. It was chopped meat mixed with sweet ginger sauce and green beans.

Totally disgusting.

So one night I e-mailed Bennett a picture of it. I didn't think he'd believe that it really existed.

After that, he started e-mailing me pictures of his dinner. We called it the "Dinner Diaries."

And in a way, it helped me feel close to him. Close to his life outside Seagate. Even when the photos weren't of anything exciting—boiled hot dogs or spaghetti with butter.

But then one day I wanted to stop doing it. It felt weird knowing about his home life in Boston.

I liked Seagate Bennett. I liked that, in a way, he only existed in the summer. In this special place. And the more I talked to Bennett during the year, the more nervous I got. I worried that there was this whole other part of him that I didn't know and wouldn't like in the same way. I worried about being more than friends and what that meant. I worried about what it would be like to kiss him.

If our friendship was year-round, if we talked all the time, that meant it was something deeper. And that seemed scary.

Maybe spending time with him for the swim lessons would help me understand how I felt.

I needed to find out.

After a few more rainy days, the weather took a turn for the better. We told all our clients to meet us at Dog Beach at ten in the morning so we could officially start the summer of doggie day care.

"You're going to be reunited with your friends," I tell Marilyn Monroe on the walk over. Truthfully, I think she's been a little bored. We all have. Rainy Seagate isn't as fun as sunny Seagate.

Her tail wags as soon as I tell her; she starts to walk a little faster.

Calvin and Claire are already at Dog Beach when Marilyn Monroe and I get there.

Claire's eyes are red. And Calvin greets us in an extra happy tone, as if he's trying to convince us of something.

I keep thinking about Claire's sad statement: *We were a*

family once. It's so simple and yet so complicated at the same time. I don't know what their future will be.

"Claire, I'm here if you want to talk," I whisper. I should have said it to both of them, but Calvin has never really opened up to me about anything before, so it seems like a strange thing to say to him, too. I still feel odd about my urge to hug him the other day.

"Actually, can we?" She perks up a bit. "Let's walk over to the water together."

Marilyn Monroe traipses along with us even though I take her off her leash. I'm convinced she understands what's going on. She's kind of like Danish in that way—my old dog who passed away two years ago. Danish always seemed to show concern when someone was sad, along with the many other human characteristics she had.

"What's going on?" I ask Claire.

"Well, it just stinks. The whole thing stinks. At first my mom told me she and my dad were going to try to work things out. But now it seems like they're not."

My shoulders tense up. "What do you mean?"

"Well, my dad just got his own apartment in Manhattan." She pauses, sniffling. "That's how I know."

"Really?"

"Yeah. We found out today. My mom was talking to my grandfather at the kitchen table this morning, and I over-heard them. It's only a two-bedroom. Calvin and I will have to share a room when we're there, or one of us will have to sleep on the couch." She rubs her eye with a sleeve of her sweatshirt. "I wonder how long she was going to wait to tell me. So now I'm not talking to her."

It seems as if Claire wants to say more, so I stay quiet and wait for her to continue.

"I didn't even want to come to Dog Beach today, but there wasn't anything for me to do at my grandfather's house, and I didn't want to let you down. I don't really want to do anything, but I also don't want to be alone. I can't even explain it. My brain is like a bowl of oatmeal."

We get to the very edge of the sand, and the water washes over our feet. "Well, I know this won't really help things, but I'm glad you're here."

I reach out to give her a hug, and she puts her head on my shoulder. "It's just so unfair. I mean, they always fought and stuff, but I didn't think it would come to this. I thought we'd always stick together."

"Well, is there a chance it's just a separation?" I ask. "It may not be permanent."

"It's permanent." She rubs her eyes some more. "I keep thinking it's a nightmare, and I'll wake up and it will be okay. Back to the way it used to be."

I nod.

"I want to pretend it's not happening. Am I making any sense?"

"You are," I say. "You really are."

She looks grateful for the reassurance. "I'm not the kind

of person who gives up. So I figured there would always be a way to work it out," she says.

"You're *not* the kind of person who gives up," I tell her. "You're really not. But I guess you don't have control over this."

I think that's the hardest thing in life: not having control over something. Lately, everything seems to be changing, and there's nothing I can do about it.

"And Calvin seems okay with it," Claire says. "He acts like he doesn't care."

"Well, I mean, maybe—"

Our conversation gets interrupted when Paul and Andi arrive with Atticus and Rascal. The dogs sprint onto the sand and start wagging their tails as soon as they see Marilyn Monroe. Soon all three of them are running back and forth on the beach, as if the moment they've been waiting for has finally arrived.

They're exactly like the kids on Seagate Island. Waiting all year for the summer day when they're reunited with their favorite friends.

"So, these two are all set," Paul tells us. "We put some extra treats in a little baggie on the bench, but they should be good to go. There's also some dry food in there if they seem to be starving."

"Got it," I reply.

Everyone else arrives in the next five minutes: Potato Salad the collie, Tabby the beagle, and a new Portuguese water dog named Oreo.

"Sorry I'm late. I had to bring Asher's lunch to him at camp. He forgot it." Bennett runs onto the sand, carrying his flip-flops. He's such a good big brother. "So, everyone's here?"

"Everyone's here!" I smile. "Well, except Lester."

As I look at all the dogs on the sand, it feels as if summer has finally started. As if all the days that led up to today were just practice.

"Do you have room for one more?" a plump lady with bright orange hair and a smallish dog on a leash calls out to me. I'm sitting on the sand with all the dogs around me; we look as if we're about to play a game of duck-duck-goose. Or I guess we could call it dog-dog-person.

I stand up, and she introduces herself.

"I'm Sylvia Adler. We just arrived on Seagate, and I heard all about your doggie day care, Remy. My husband and I bought a place down by the lighthouse, and we're very busy with renovations and construction. It's hard to have a dog around when you're knocking down walls." She shakes her head. "I've just been so worried about Ritzy. She could get sick from the dust!"

"Sure. We'd love to help." I look over at Bennett, Micayla, Calvin, and Claire, and they're sitting with the dogs now, petting them and chatting. The dogs are in good hands, and Claire looks much better than she did before. It's amazing what dogs can do for someone's mood. Even a few seconds with a dog makes you immediately calmer and more relaxed.

"Tell us a little bit about your dog." I motion for the others to come over, so I can introduce them. I think it's really important that the owners meet all of us.

"Her name is Ritzy, short for Ritz-Carlton, my favorite hotel." She smiles. "I'm a world traveler, and it's the only hotel I'll stay at. Anyway, you can call her Ritzy, or RC. She's a Jack Russell terrier, and she's very friendly and smart. She gets along well with other dogs, and she loves a good tummy rub."

"Who doesn't, right?" I laugh, and Sylvia nods. She's clearly a braggy dog owner who thinks her pup is better than anyone else's. But I can't really fault her for that. Ritzy does look pretty cute and very well-behaved. It wouldn't surprise me if Ritzy's been taking doggie etiquette lessons.

The Jack Russell sits up perfectly straight, as if she's trying to impress us. Her brown ears are perked up, waiting for me to tell her something very exciting.

Ritzy's owner thanks me and says she needs to get home. "I'd better get back to my contractor. He's driving me crazy."

Bennett organizes a Frisbee game, and Ritzy joins in as if she's known all the other dogs forever.

Right then, Lester arrives. Mrs. Decsini drags the cocker spaniel across the sand like he's a kid who doesn't want to go to school.

"Lester!" I exclaim, already sensing that he needs a little extra TLC.

"Hello, Remy," Mrs. Decsini says. "He's having a tough summer. I don't know what's bugging him lately."

"Really? I'm sorry to hear that. Tell me about his year."

She stops to think for a second. "His year was fine. Nothing unusual. Lots of good times with his best doggie friend, Turbo the poodle. We took him to all the kids' sporting events. Everything was great." She shrugs. "Oh, except for one thing. We tried to give him some of his old toys for Christmas. Usually we go all out, but it was an expensive year." She looks sad all of a sudden. "We even had to sell our piano to complete some necessary home renovations." She looks at me and shrugs again. "I have no idea why I'm going into any of this. But anyway, for Christmas, we wrapped up his old things, toys he hadn't played with in a while." She shakes her head. "He totally knew. He even growled at us. Come to think of it, that may have been when his mood changed."

I try not to laugh. People don't like old gifts, and neither do dogs.

"Hopefully some time with you and the other dogs will help," she tells me. "We rented a house with a few other families this summer. Maybe that's the problem. Maybe he's grown antisocial in his old age."

"I see." I bend down to pet Lester. "He's in good hands with us."

"Good luck." She kisses the top of his head. "Hope he behaves himself."

"Lester," I say as soon as his owner-mom is far enough

away that I can talk to him in private, "I'm so excited to see you. We're going to have a great summer!"

He gives me a look as if he's not sure he believes me.

"First things first," I tell him, and I look around to make sure the gate is closed. "Let's get you free. I know leashes bug you, and you're safe at Dog Beach." I unclip him, and he makes a run for it.

"Lester!" I yell, and I instantly regret my kindness and sensitivity. He took advantage of it, and now I'm sprinting across the beach like a maniac, running after him.

Dogs can be classic "give 'em an inch, and they'll take a mile" creatures.

I catch up to him and put him back on the leash, and we walk slowly back to the group.

We can turn Lester's summer around and make him happy again. I know it. He's stubborn and routine-oriented, true. But we can handle that.

I guess we all like things our own way sometimes.

The most important thing is for me to figure out why he's unhappy and why he wanted to run away in the first place.

I stay up late researching dog behavior online
—especially that of cocker spaniels—so I can better understand Lester. Running a doggie day camp isn't only about
good times and quality supervision. It's about taking the time
to really understand the dogs. Apparently cocker spaniels
are very sensitive. It's important to pay attention to how we
discipline them and how we talk to them with our hands.
Maybe his owners don't realize that something they're doing
might be causing him to act out.

I'm exhausted the next morning and practically falling
asleep on the bench while trying to set up all the different
dogs' lunches, when someone startles me.

"Are you Remy?" the person asks.

I look up, nod, and pretend to be wide awake. "Uh-huh."

"I'm Josh Gold. I hoped I'd find you here," he says. He's

not a teenager, but he's not an adult. Must be a college student. He's wearing plaid shorts and an SGI SWEETS 2001 T-shirt. Clearly a longtime Seagater.

"Hi, Josh," I say. "Nice to meet you."

Maybe he's part of the beach crew this year, making sure we're cleaning up after the dogs, keeping the area clean?

"So, my buddies and I are part of an improv troupe," he says. "You know what improv is?"

Does he think I'm six years old? Of course I do.

I glare at him. "Yeah, I know what improv is."

He laughs. "Okay, well, great. So my troupe and I are spending the summer on Seagate, running some kids' acting classes and working on our skills so we can enter this national competition. We're called the Improvimaniacs."

"Uh-huh."

I can feel Micayla, Bennett, Claire, and Calvin staring at me from the edge of the water. It's not every day a college kid comes to talk to me.

"I was told you run a day care program for dogs?" he asks, looking a bit confused, as if it's one of the craziest things he's ever heard of.

"Yeah." I laugh. It always feels funny when people know about us. As if we're a real business.

"We want to get some animals involved in our routines," he says. "We really want to step up our game. And the dogs will make everything so spontaneous."

"Okay . . ." I cover my mouth to avoid cracking up. This feels too silly to be true.

"So we wondered if we could come hang with your dogs some days and practice with them," he tells me. "While they're in doggie day care. It can be kind of like their theater elective?" He smiles broadly, as if he's trying to convince me.

"I'll think about it," I tell him, still trying not to laugh as I imagine the dogs acting onstage. "This is only our second day, and we're trying to get the dogs situated." I pause. "But it sounds like a fun idea."

I see Ritzy trying to steal a ball from Rascal. Lester is at the very edge of Dog Beach, about to make a run for it again, and Marilyn Monroe keeps looking over at me as if she's bored. I should probably end this conversation for now.

"Thanks for thinking about it, Remy," he says and gives me his phone number. "Oh, and I forgot to mention, I'm planning to be a vet. I don't know very much yet, but I do know some things about dogs."

"Cool," I say.

If he knows some things about being a vet, he should know that I really need to get back to the dogs!

"So, how 'bout this? I'll bring the other members of the troupe by tomorrow, and we can explain what we were thinking about, in terms of getting the dogs into our act."

"Okay. How many of you are there?" I ask.

"Well, there are four of us."

"Okay."

Only on Seagate Island would a college kid come to talk to a twelve-year-old running a doggie day care program. That's the magic of Seagate, right there in a nutshell.

"What was that all about?" Bennett asks when I get back to the group. "It seemed like a really intense conversation."

"Not much, really," I tell him. "It was kinda odd. You know that improv troupe we've seen running the acting classes in the stadium?"

Everyone nods, and I tell them what Josh said about getting the dogs involved, their competition, and everything else.

"Josh is a genius," Bennett says. "He goes to Yale." He throws a Frisbee to Atticus.

"Okay . . ." I'm not sure what that really has to do with this improv situation, but it only goes to prove that Bennett knows every single person on Seagate Island. "Anyway, they're coming by tomorrow to hang out with the dogs."

"Sounds cool," Calvin says. "I mean, improv can be really funny." He pauses and turns to his sister. "Right, Claire?"

She rolls her eyes and walks away.

Calvin sighs. "Well, *I* think it's cool. She does, too. We went on a cruise once, and there was an improv show. Claire was picked out of the audience to participate."

He runs down the beach to continue the Frisbee game with Bennett.

I notice that Claire's crying again, but Calvin is acting as if everything is fine. Maybe that's the key word: *acting.* His parents' pending divorce has got to be upsetting him, too.

I walk over to Claire. "How are you?" I ask, even though it seems like the dumbest question in the world.

"Bad. I saw my mom crying again."

"Really?" I answer. I want to be there for Claire, but I don't know what to say.

"Yeah, and she's not a crier. I mean, the only other time I saw her cry was when my grandma died. She didn't even cry when she broke her foot or got stung by five bees."

"That's a hard thing to see," I say. "I'm really sorry this is happening to you."

Everything I say sounds wrong after it comes out of my mouth. Maybe there's someone I can turn to for guidance. I thought about asking Bennett for advice, but now it seems easier to talk to someone else. I've spent time studying dog behavior, but I guess I need to spend time studying human behavior, too.

"I just realized that this may be our last Seagate summer. We'll probably have to spend summers with my dad from now on."

"Really? No! You just got here."

"I know. Everything about this totally stinks," she says. "I really don't know what's going to happen."

"Let's not think about the future; things can always change," I tell her. "But I know what you mean. I always want to know how things are going to end up. Not knowing is the worst part."

"Exactly," she says, and this makes me feel good. Maybe I'm making some sense; maybe I actually understand how she's feeling.

I continue. "And I think you're right about getting used to the new way of things. It's like when Micayla and her sister and brother, Ivy and Zane, became year-rounders here. There was so much buildup and tension, and then, once it was settled, it turned out fine."

"Remy." Claire gives me a cold stare. "These two things are not the same. At all. You can't compare Micayla's living year-round in a beach town to my parents' getting divorced. Come on."

"No, I—"

Claire stands up and walks away, and I'm left feeling like the worst friend in the world.

"Claire seems so sad today," Micayla says a few minutes later, carrying over Tabby's water bowl so she can fill it up. "Did anything new happen?"

"No, I don't think so. Just the usual stuff," I tell her. I don't want to rehash my conversation with Claire and how I messed it up.

"By the way," Micayla says, "I don't want to freak you out, but I think Calvin likes you."

I gasp. "What?"

At that exact moment, all the dogs seem to go crazy. Marilyn Monroe starts running in circles. Potato Salad and Oreo swim way too far out, and Bennett has to rescue them. Tabby, Rascal, and Atticus all start growling as if they're in a giant fight. And Ritzy seems to have tummy troubles.

And then there's Lester, huddled under a lounge chair, the way he's been for the past half hour. Maybe Ritzy is freaking him out. He seems to shy away from her.

"We have to focus on the dogs," I tell her. "But I need more details. Obviously."

"Right. Let's talk later."

The whole time I'm wrangling the dogs and trying to solve all their problems, I'm thinking about what Micayla just told me. Could it possibly be true?

It feels like the most terrible yet exciting news.

I don't know what to do with this information. I came here this summer thinking everything would be perfect: I liked Bennett, the doggie day care business was going to be easy-breezy, I was going to be a great help to Claire, and we were all going to have the best summer ever.

But now Claire thinks I don't understand her, Calvin might like me, and the weather is totally unpredictable, with a storm possibly on the summer horizon.

And a college improv troupe wants to recruit our dogs?

Nothing makes sense anymore.

It feels like the summer I was eight, and, without realizing what I was doing, I swam out too far. The ocean started to get choppy, and the waves got bigger and bigger, crashing over my head. And one of the lifeguards had to dive in to help me.

That's how I feel right now. I swam out too far. I need to be rescued.

"Did you ever know anyone whose parents got divorced?" I ask my dad over dinner. My mom is at book club tonight, and Dad and I decided to walk to Frederick's Fish and eat on their roof deck.

I'd never tell Mom this, but I love the nights she has book club. Sometimes it's nice to have Dad all to myself. Mom has a tendency to ask too many questions when I turn to her for advice. Dad sits quietly and listens. He only chimes in with a question when absolutely necessary.

"Yes, a few people, actually." He takes a bite of his fish sandwich and looks at me with wide eyes, as if I should continue.

"Well, how did you help them?" I ask, and then decide to rephrase my question. "I guess what I'm asking is, did you ever have a friend whose parents were going through a divorce, and you didn't know how to help her?"

Dad wipes his mouth with a napkin. "I guess all you can really do is be there for your friend and listen. Let her know that you care."

"Maybe," I say. "I just feel like I should be doing more. Helping more. You know?"

He nods. "I know. You like to help. But sometimes just being around is helping. Sometimes less is more."

He's probably right, but I wanted something concrete, something that I could actually do to help Claire.

It feels terrible to know that you can't fix something. I can't fix how Claire is feeling, just like she can't fix the problems her parents are having.

But there has to be something I can do.

Later that night, I toss and turn, unable to fall asleep. Marilyn Monroe is getting frustrated, too, whimpering every time I move. She hops off the bed and chooses to sleep on my window seat. Normally she puts up with my erratic sleep behavior. Not tonight. I guess she's too tired from her big day on Dog Beach.

When I really can't take the insomnia anymore, I decide to text Micayla and see if she's up. It's pretty common for both of us to have trouble sleeping on the same nights. I'm grateful that we're on good terms again and she's not feeling left out anymore. At least my friendship with Micayla is one thing I can feel good about right now.

Are you up?

I wait for a response, then hop out of bed to go to the

bathroom, and when I get back, there's a text message on my screen.

Yes, unfortunately. Call me.

I tiptoe out of my room because I don't want to wake Marilyn Monroe. I go out onto the back porch to call Micayla. One of the zillion wonderful things about Seagate is that I can go outside even in the middle of the night and Mom and Dad don't worry. We don't have an alarm that will go off. I don't need to take an elevator, or even a flight of stairs. I can go right outside and breathe in the ocean air at any hour of the day or night.

It's the best thing in the world.

"What's up?" Micayla says.

"Can't sleep. I dunno. What about you?"

She sighs. "Me neither. My sister and my mom had this huge fight, and it's been bugging me."

"What was the fight about?" I ask.

"Something boring, like studying abroad. My mom thinks my sister should consider it, but my sister doesn't want to because of what her friends are doing, or something like that. I don't really know." She pauses. "I hate it when they fight."

"I'm sorry," I say. "That sounds horrible."

"What's on your mind? Why can't you sleep?" she asks me.

"Well, a few things. I guess partly the whole Claire situation. I feel like she's going through such a hard time, and

I don't know how to help. And then there's what you said before."

"About Calvin?" She groans. "I shouldn't have told you. I knew you'd freak out."

"Freak out?" I say way too loudly for almost one in the morning. "I'm not freaking out. I'm just thinking about it."

"Right now you're freaking out because I *said* you were freaking out." She laughs. "See what I mean?"

"No." I roll my eyes, wishing she could see that through the phone. "Just tell me why you think that. Okay?"

"I overheard him telling Bennett."

My heart pounds. "What do you mean, he told Bennett? Like, he said it flat out?"

"Kind of. I mean, it was in boy talk. They said 'dude' a lot and 'yeah, she's cool' and that kind of thing."

"And what did Bennett say?" I ask.

She waits a second to answer. "He was just, like, 'Cool, go for it.'"

"Really?" My entire heart slips away like an ice cream cone dropped on a hot sidewalk.

If Bennett doesn't care, then he doesn't like me the way I thought he did. I know I wasn't sure how I felt about him, but it still stings to know he doesn't like *me*.

My mind spins in circles like the spiral paintings we used to do on the boardwalk.

Micayla yawns. "Yeah, but you know how guys are. Don't stress about it. I probably shouldn't have told you."

"No, it's okay. Mic, I'm feeling sleepy now, actually. See you tomorrow morning. Ten o'clock, Dog Beach, okay?"

"Okay," she says. "Nighty-night."

I can't believe Bennett would say that to Calvin. I don't know how I'll face him tomorrow. And I don't know how I'll face Calvin, either. Plus, I'm worried about Claire.

There are so many problems surrounding the people on our dog-sitting team, and I don't know how to fix any of them.

I'm so tired the next morning that a whole day
with the dogs seems like running a marathon in high heels.

Bennett texts me and suggests a swimming lesson for later in the day, but I tell him no. I don't have the energy to swim. More important, I don't have the energy to worry about a swimming lesson with Bennett.

"Come on, Mari," I say. She's tired, too, and frankly kind of annoyed that I kept her up last night. She growls at me, which she never, ever does.

"Stop. I'm sorry. I had things on my mind," I say to her.

Her growl turns into a whimper, and she nudges my calf with her nose as we walk to Dog Beach.

"Thanks for understanding," I tell her.

We get to Dog Beach, and Calvin, Claire, and a few of the dogs are already there. I sit down on the bench with Marilyn

Monroe and take longer than necessary to get out her treats and her special water bowl. I don't want to go over to the others. I don't know how to act. And then it occurs to me—I wonder if Claire knows that Calvin likes me. I mean, if it's even true that he likes me.

It seems too crazy to be true. I don't think Micayla would lie about it, but it just doesn't seem to make sense.

I'm filling up Marilyn Monroe's bowl with the spring water she likes (she's very particular) when Claire comes over.

"Hey," she says.

"Hey." I look up and smile. "How are you?"

"Good," she says. "I don't want you to always look at me like I'm about to cry. Okay?"

"I didn't realize I was doing that. Sorry."

"You don't always do it," she clarifies. "But sometimes you do. And it's annoying."

"Got it." The truth is, now I feel like *I'm* about to cry. Hearing that I'm doing something annoying feels like I just poked a thumbtack into my finger.

"Anyway, what's going on with you?" she asks.

I look over at Marilyn Monroe, who has fallen asleep on the sand. "We both had insomnia last night," I explain.

"I'll bring over a lounge chair for you," she says. "I can take the early shift."

"That's kind of you, but I think I should be alert and ready for the clients. And remember what happened last time we lounged too long?"

She looks at me, confused.

"The whole Marilyn Monroe Mornings incident." Last summer Mari got too wild at Mornings one day, and let's just say that she was not welcomed back. "We were too groggy from sleep to think clearly!"

Claire cracks up. "Okay, well, maybe you need a latte or something."

Claire's one of those kids who drinks coffee sometimes, and I've tried it, but I don't really like the taste. Maybe a Coke, though. I'll definitely need a Coke later.

Claire goes to greet Rascal and Atticus when Paul and Andi drop them off, and I close my eyes for a second. When I open them, Calvin is sitting next to me.

"Hey," he says. "Slacking again?"

"Again?" I glare at him. "I'm not sure I know what you're talking about."

"I'm kidding," he says. "What's up?"

I don't know where to look, where to focus my eyes. Anywhere but on Calvin. "Not much, really." I force an awkward smile. "I wanted to talk to you, actually. And it seems like it's never just the two of us. I'm worried about Claire."

He sighs. "Yeah, she's having a tough time."

I wait for him to say more, or to say how he's feeling, but he doesn't.

"How are you doing?" I ask.

He gives me a look, as if there's absolutely no reason for me to be asking that. "Fine. I'm fine."

I get the sense that he wants to put an end to this conversation. This may have been the longest chat I've ever had with Calvin, and it feels impossible to keep it going.

"I got you something, and I keep forgetting to give it to you," he says. "My dad took me to this used bookstore before we came to Seagate. I saw a book there that I knew you had to have."

"What is it? I can't take the suspense."

He pulls a tiny book out of the pocket of his cargo shorts and hands it to me. Its title is *Understanding Your Dog: A Breed-by-Breed Guide*.

"Wow, thanks."

"I figured it would be good for you to have. You know, because we have some new clients and stuff. This will give us some insight into the different breeds and everything."

"Yeah, definitely." I flip through the book. "Maybe it'll help us figure out why Lester is going through some kind of emotional crisis. Oh, look at this! A quiz! We can take it and find out which breed is right for us."

He laughs. "You can become a dog matchmaker. You'll help people find their ideal canine companion!"

"You're totally on to something! If my doggie day care business doesn't work out, I'll try dog matchmaking."

I start asking Calvin the quiz questions, and the awkwardness melts away. It feels normal to be hanging out with him. Fun, even.

And then Claire comes over to us with her hands on her hips and says, "What are you guys laughing about? You sound like hyenas."

"Nothing. I just gave Remy that book I found when Dad took us to that cool used bookstore in Amenia."

"Oh. Yeah. Whatever." She rolls her eyes. "Dad will probably never take us anywhere ever again. We should have appreciated it more when he took us places."

Calvin digs the toe of his sneaker into the sand. "Dramatic much? I'm sure he'll take us other places."

"I wouldn't be so sure," Claire says, and the awkwardness comes back. I don't know what to say. "Anyway, are you guys gonna help watch the dogs? Or you're on vacation here? Because Lester and Ritzy are growling at each other again, Oreo won't stop peeing, and Rascal just ate a whole salad of seaweed. And, frankly, Marilyn Monroe looks really bored by it all."

Her last two points don't surprise me. Rascal is always eating the wrong things. The Newfoundland manages to find a way into the other dogs' food, even though he has pretty specific dietary restrictions. And Marilyn Monroe is always bored when I'm not around. She needs constant entertainment.

It was so sweet of Calvin to bring me that book. And it has me thinking about something else: he brought up his dad to me. He never does that.

The three of us walk over to the dogs, and the situation is

worse than I expected. Rascal is lying on the ground, whimpering. His stomach bobs in and out.

"I think he's dehydrated. I'm trying to get him to drink, but he won't," Micayla says. "We should take him home."

"What did he eat?" I ask. "Besides the seaweed?"

Micayla clenches her teeth as if she doesn't want to tell me. "He got into some of Atticus's treats. He can't have those, because he has some kind of gluten allergy."

"Dogs have gluten allergies, too?" Claire says. "That's ridiculous!"

"No, it's true," Micayla explains. She's really taken ownership of Rascal and Atticus this summer. I think she feels closer to them since Paul was her teacher last year. "I'm going to call Mr. Jennings and Andi."

"No, don't!" I yell, and then I lower my voice. "They'll think we're not capable of taking care of the dogs. We can't have that. We need to handle this ourselves."

"Well, you should have been paying more attention," Micayla says, annoyed at me. "You were on the bench relaxing, and then this happened. Bennett and I were here by ourselves with all the dogs."

"Hey! What am I? Chopped liver?" Claire says, and then she starts laughing. "My grandpa says that all the time. I don't even get it, but it's funny."

"You weren't paying attention, either," Micayla reminds her. "Sorry, but it's true."

"Okay, guys, calm down," Bennett says. "Let's think about

this. I'll try to get Rascal to drink some water from his bowl. Things will be easier to figure out if we stay calm."

I take a deep breath and rub Rascal's back. And then I remember: Josh!

The improv troupe guy. He's studying at Yale to be a vet. He knows things about dogs. He said so himself.

"Rascal seems really weak. He can barely lift up his head." Bennett looks up at me. "I don't think I've ever seen him like this."

"Remy, I don't think we should ignore this," Micayla says.

She's right. I messed up, and I need to handle it.

Atticus looks worried, pacing back and forth on the sand. All the dogs are concerned, actually. They're hovering around the Newfoundland, and they won't do any of their activities. Oreo keeps nudging Rascal with his nose, and he doesn't even respond.

"Okay, we have to do something," I admit finally. "That kid Josh said he knows some stuff about dogs. Maybe he can help."

Thankfully, Josh answers his phone. He's finishing up breakfast at Mornings. He says he'll come right over.

"All right, what do we have here?" Josh says in a jokey tone as he runs down the beach a minute later. Maybe I shouldn't have called him. Maybe he really doesn't know anything.

We explain the situation.

"Two things are happening here," Josh informs us. "He has an upset stomach, and he's dehydrated."

Duh. We know that.

"I'll be right back!" He starts running across the sand.

"Wait! Don't leave! What if something happens?" I yell, not meaning to. My heart is racing, and everything feels out of control right now.

"Two minutes," Josh calls over his shoulder. "I'll be back in two minutes."

We stand around Rascal and keep putting his water bowl in front of him. Micayla rubs his belly, and Calvin tells him that everything is going to be okay. Claire and Bennett take care of the other dogs.

"Oh, this is so terrible," I say over and over again. "How did this happen?"

"It's going to be okay," Calvin says. To me this time, and not to Rascal. "Really, it'll be okay. Humans get upset stomachs. Dogs do, too. That's all."

At this moment, I want to give Calvin some kind of medal. He knows exactly what to say. He doesn't even seem frazzled or stressed.

He stays focused and strong. His face is serious but reassuring.

"Are you sure?" I ask him.

"Yes. Don't worry. And Josh wouldn't have left if he thought Rascal was really in danger. He'll be back, and everything will be fine."

I look at Calvin. His shorts are frayed on the bottoms, and his polo shirt has a bleach stain under the collar. But all I see is how cute he looks. I don't know why I never realized how amazing he is.

Josh hustles back to us. "Okay, I have some ice. This will help. And I also got a scoop of lemon sorbet from Josie Puler-witz, the owner of Sundae Best. I don't know why, but it's been known to soothe even the most troubled of tummies."

"Really?" I ask.

"It's true," he says. "Josie gave it to me for the first time when I was six years old. She promises that it's the best stomach remedy out there. And I believe it. It's helped me more times than I can count." He pauses. "Sorry, that may have been too much information." He laughs.

Josh gives Rascal the ice slowly, one cube at a time. The Newfoundland is reluctant at first to take any. But then, little by little, he licks and consumes the cubes. I'm not sure if that's considered eating or drinking, but whatever it is, he is rehydrating, and I'm grateful for that!

"See? I told you everything would be okay," Calvin says, putting his arm around me for a second and then pulling it away.

"You were right."

He smiles.

"Thanks so much, Josh."

"No problem." Josh gives Rascal a tiny taste of lemon sor-bet to see if he wants some. The big dog turns away, but then he slowly takes a few licks.

We all decide that we'll tell Andi and Paul about Rascal's

stomach problem when they come to pick up their dogs. For now, though, Rascal is happy and playing again.

And I feel closer to Calvin than ever before. I guess that's what happens when you go through a crisis together.

After the Rascal incident, things seem to calm down a little bit. At least in the doggie day care department. We even have a new sign! Mr. Brookfield is friends with Carl McMann from the Seagate Signs Company. He's the one who makes all the beachy-looking signs that people put up in front of their houses. They have Adirondack chairs on them, or reclining lounges. The signs practically breathe sun, sand, and sea. They say things like GONE SWIMMING, or LIFE IS BETTER AT THE BEACH.

So, as a surprise, Mr. Brookfield asked Carl to make us a sign to hang at the entrance of Dog Beach. I'm not sure it's really allowed, but I don't think anyone is going to force us to take it down.

It says SEAGATE ISLAND DOGGIE DAY CAMP, so I guess that's our name now. I like it. And I love that we have a sign. We're official, and people take us seriously.

But things also change after the Rascal incident because Josh and I bonded over the crisis that day. His acting troupe stops by in the afternoons to hang with the dogs and practice some improv exercises. For example, one of the troupe members will start doing a random thing, like jumping, and then the others will join in and jump around, too, which leads them to doing other silly movements. They try to include the dogs whenever possible, which causes the actors to have to react or adapt their actions in some funny way. Sometimes the dogs are into it. Sometimes they're not. I guess that's what improv is all about. You never really know how it's going to turn out, but you have to roll with the punches.

But even though things seem calmer in the Doggie Day Camp department, so much still feels crazy.

Every morning, I wake up and run outside immediately to check the ocean and see how the weather is. I don't know why I do it, since it's impossible to predict the path of a hurricane very far in advance. But the sea makes me feel calmer. I know it's crazy, but when I'm out there, I talk to the ocean in my head.

I tell the ocean to stay calm; I tell any possible storms to stay away.

There was one time, years and years ago, when Grandma had to evacuate the island and come stay with us in Manhattan. She had no idea what was going on in Seagate because the whole island lost power, and everyone was gone. She stayed with us for two weeks and didn't even know if her house would be there when she got back. It ultimately needed a new roof, and the whole first floor was destroyed. But it could have been worse. She said so herself.

Marilyn Monroe and I hustle toward Dog Beach, even though we have at least an hour before the other dogs arrive. Claire, Calvin, Micayla, Bennett, and even Mason are doing all the pickups today. They offered, and I didn't argue with them. And since Mason has been so busy with his Italian lessons, it will be nice to see him for a change.

I try to study everyone I see on the way to the beach. Are they worried about a storm, too? Do they seem stressed? But to me, everyone looks like their normal, happy Seagate Island selves.

"See, Mari? Everything's going to be fine," I tell her as we're walking onto Dog Beach. "I don't understand why we worry about things we can't control. Things will be the same whether we worry or not."

I know all this, and yet I still worry. It doesn't make sense.

Mari barks her happy *I agree* bark and plops down next to me on the sand. She stretches her paws out in front of her and closes her eyes. She's tired from listening to all of my rambles, I guess. Either that or she's been up at night worrying, like I have.

Soon everyone else arrives. Claire's eyes are red, as they usually are these days. I try to study Calvin, to see what he does when he sees me. Does he get nervous? Does he straighten out his shirt or anything?

But nope. Nothing. He just nudges his head in my direction, the way he says hi most of the time. Then he goes to play Frisbee with Ritzy, Oreo, Atticus, and Rascal. They're a crew this summer, and they can't be separated.

Ritzy looks so small compared to the others. Sometimes I can't even see her little brown and white Jack Russell body. It gets hidden by the bigger dogs.

"So, what's up, Rem?" Bennett asks. "Gonna bail on your swimming lesson again?"

I glare at him. "I only bailed once."

"Whatever." He puts his hands on his hips and does a fake-angry pose.

I know he's joking with me, but I can barely look at him. Why does he care about missing our swimming lessons when he didn't care that Calvin liked me?

The boys all go to handle the dogs for a moment, while the girls take a break and do some serious lounging. It's a new thing we started, giving one another a few minutes off.

"I don't know what to do about Mason," Micayla says. "He's just kind of needy lately. Like, he asked me if I'd quiz him on Italian."

"What?" Claire scoffs. "Are you serious?"

"Yeah." She makes a face. "I mean, come on. No one wants to quiz anyone on anything in the summer."

"Are you two even together?" Claire asks.

Claire always has a way of saying exactly what she's thinking. Sometimes it hurts people's feelings, but she does it anyway. It seems to have gotten worse this summer, but I think it's because of everything she's dealing with at home.

"Never mind. Forget I even brought this up." Micayla gets up from the sand. She walks away, to the dogs and the boys.

Claire raises her eyebrows at me. "What was that all about?"

"They *are* together," I remind her. "You knew that."

"I did not. They barely even hang out. And Mason rarely helps at Dog Beach anymore." She huffs. "Can I have the day off? I'm really tired."

"Whatever you need to do," I say.

She looks at me, waiting for me to say more. Maybe I should be more supportive. But right now Lester is twisted up in some seaweed because he was trying to run away from Ritzy, and the rest of the dogs are barking because they're starving and waiting for their lunch.

I have no idea how to balance the dog responsibilities with my friend responsibilities. But I'll have to find a way.

It's gray out, but Josh and the Improvimaniacs practice with the dogs on the beach. It's so funny that it takes my mind off the gloomy weather and my gloomy mood.

Right now they're pretending Oreo is a professor and the four actors are in a class with the rest of the dogs. It's cracking us up, because Oreo keeps falling asleep on the sand and Josh's friend Liat has to wake him up over and over again.

And then it starts pouring. Not raining. Pouring. Thick, clumpy raindrops that pelt the dogs' fur and make it hard for us to see.

"Guys, come on!" Josh yells to us.

"What?" I yell. It's hard to hear through the rain.

He yells back, "Follow me. Grab the dogs! Quick!"

So we gather up the dogs and all their stuff as fast as we can. Ritzy's such a slow walker that Calvin picks her up and runs with her. We follow Josh and the Improvimaniacs until we're standing in front of the old Seagate Hotel.

"Come on in."

Josh really wants us to bring the dogs in there? Dripping, wet-dog-smelling dogs? I can't believe it. But I'm too drenched to argue.

Once the dogs are inside, they run around the lobby and check out the place. They sniff every corner. They're as confused as we are.

"What's going on?" I ask. "We're allowed to be in here?"

"Yeah, my family owns this place," Josh tells us. "It's empty this summer while my mom and her crazy sisters figure out what they want to do with it. It was my grandfather's place, and since he passed away, they haven't decided if they should sell it or not. Anyway, we're staying here this summer, running the improv and theater activities for the kids and looking after the place."

"Really?" I ask. "Just you and your friends?"

He nods. "Yup. You seem shocked."

I look around to *my* friends, but they're with the dogs. I *am* shocked. I can't imagine having an entire hotel to ourselves.

"So, you've spent a lot of summers on Seagate?" I ask him.

"I visited a bunch, but I never spent the whole summer. My mom and her sisters are so distraught about my grandfather dying that they didn't have the strength to come here or figure out what to do with the hotel. So I said I'd come and sort things out, if I was allowed to bring the Improvimaniacs with me."

"I see."

"And it's been so rainy, we've been indoors way more than I like to be," he tells me. "So it's good to have the extra space."

"Right."

"It was the first place I could think to take you guys when it started raining." He cracks his neck. "Must be tough for you guys, too. What do you do with the dogs when it rains?"

"Nothing," I say. "They just stay home for the most part, where they get bored. Plus, we make a lot less money."

"Wow." Josh laughs. "You're quite the entrepreneur."

"No, no, that's not what I mean." I crack up, picturing myself in some kind of fancy suit, working on Wall Street. "We're trying to raise money, to save an animal shelter in Manhattan that's in danger of closing."

"That's awesome," Josh says.

I shrug. "Thanks."

"Well, now you can bring the dogs here when it rains," he says. "It's just an empty space for the most part. As you can see." He looks around. "Hope you don't need to, though. I hope the weather takes a turn for the better."

I nod and look around the place. It's gigantic. We're standing in what used to be the lobby, but everything's gone except for the old concierge desk. The carpet has been pulled up, revealing worn wooden floors. And there's a bay window at the back with a window seat.

I remember my grandma telling me a few years ago that when she was in her twenties, everyone would come here to the hotel for a fun night out. There's a picture of her and Grandpa sitting on that window seat. They're all dressed up, looking into each other's eyes. It's one of my favorite photos. They look like movie stars, the most beautiful people I've ever seen.

I wonder if she was friends with Josh's grandpa. I bet she was.

"It's a great space," I say. "It's so big, and the high ceilings are amazing, along with the view, of course."

"Yeah, it's great," he says. "I'd like to keep it in the family, but I think my mom just wants to move on."

Josh goes to find the rest of the troupe, and I walk over to help with the dogs.

"So we can just hang out here?" Micayla asks me. I tell her the whole story about the hotel and Josh's grandpa.

She listens but then changes the subject. "Everything seems crazy today. Claire is crying. Bennett and Calvin keep arguing about what teams are going to make the Super Bowl, even though it's July! Even the dogs are acting nuts."

I look around. Things seem moderately calm to me.

"I don't get it," I say. "The dogs are all lounging."

"They're fine right now. But I didn't even have a chance to tell you what happened with Lester this morning."

"What happened?" I ask.

"He kept trying to run away when I picked him up, even though I called him to come back a hundred times. Then he hopped onto someone's lap outside Breakfast on the Board-walk and took a bite of the woman's egg and cheese sandwich. And he can't even have dairy!"

"For real?"

"Yes, Remy. I don't know what's gotten into him. He's clearly struggling with something." She looks right into my eyes. "And you, you're struggling with something, too. I can tell. Your mind is in a hundred different places." She puts her hands on my shoulders and tries to get me to focus.

She's right. No matter how hard I try to pretend that I have everything figured out, Micyala can tell when I don't.

"Okay." I take a deep breath. *Focus, Remy, focus.* Right now I need to be here, helping with the dogs, helping my friends. Finally I come up with an indoor activity that would be good for the dogs and for relaxation.

We gather all the dogs together, and we get them to sit more or less in a circle. Maybe it's possible for us to do some doggie yoga. I try to guide them to breathe in and breathe out and breathe in and breathe out.

"This is ridiculous!" Claire says, standing up. "Dogs can't do yoga! And neither can I."

"Claire, come on," Calvin groans. "Just sit down."

"And of course dogs can do yoga," I say defensively. "Hello! Downward-facing dog?"

No one laughs, and that disappoints me a little bit.

"I need a personal day," Claire says. She's been asking for days off more and more lately, but she's still here.

"Claire," I say, though I'm a little bit tired of begging her to stick around, "please stay."

Even though my begging sounds forced, Claire sits back down. Calvin and I make eye contact, and I feel like I've swallowed a brick. And then that brick goes down my throat and into my stomach.

I don't understand how anyone can focus on anything when there's a boy you might really like who might also really like you. And there's also a boy you thought you really liked, but maybe you were wrong.

At the end of the day, we take the dogs home. Then Calvin and Bennett go to shoot hoops, and Claire, Micayla, and I walk home slowly, deciding to stop at Sundae Best on the way.

We're sitting at one of the tables in the back, drinking our milkshakes, and for the moment everything feels right.

"It's a milkshake kind of day," Josie says from where she's working at the counter. "Some days are for slurping, right?"

I don't know exactly what she means by that, but I think she's right.

It's good to be here, just us. Just the girls. Drinking milkshakes and talking about nothing all that important—which nail polish brands don't chip, when our moms will let us see R-rated movies, and the magic of the Sundae Best Surprise Scoop.

"I like to pick my flavors!" I proclaim. "I know there are

flavors I haven't tried, but I like what I like. It's weird to me that anyone would ever pick the Surprise Scoop."

"I disagree," Micayla argues. "It's fun to be surprised sometimes. Plus, I never would have known that their mango sorbet is one of the most delicious things in the world if not for the Surprise Scoop."

Claire says, "You guys, you don't need to agree. One of you likes surprises, and one of you doesn't. That's it."

"I guess," I reply. "But it still seems that the Surprise Scoop concept is—"

"Anyway . . ." Claire widens her eyes at me and turns to Micayla. "I'm sorry about what I said a few days ago. About the Mason thing. I guess I did know you guys were together. I wasn't being very nice." She looks down at her nearly empty glass.

"It's fine," Micayla mumbles. "Whatever. It's not really that big of a deal."

I don't add anything, because this seems like a conversation between Micayla and Claire. Plus, I want to leave room for Claire to talk about her situation at home if she wants to.

But instead of Claire talking about her family, Micayla continues. "So, how do I do it? Break up with Mason, I mean? Is there a nice way to break up with someone?"

I look at Claire, and then Claire looks at me. Neither of us has any experience with this situation.

"Probably not," I reply. "Breaking up is kind of a mean

thing to do, even when it's necessary, ya know? And you're going to have to see him for the rest of the summer."

"Right." Micayla slumps in her seat. "So tell me what to do. Guys, come on. Help!"

We stay at Sundae Best for another hour or so, brainstorming ideas. But none of them really seems nice.

"Bring him here," Josie says after we ask her what Micayla should do. "The Breakup Bowl is the best way to do it. A waffle-cone bowl with five scoops, whipped cream, and chocolate sauce."

"Really?" Micayla asks.

Josie nods. "It says you can still be friends. And everything is better with ice cream."

A few days later, Bennett comes over to give me a swimming lesson after a long day at Dog Beach. I keep telling myself that it will be over soon. We have only an hour left until he has to go home for dinner. I count the minutes.

"We should take advantage of the fact that it's not raining, Rem. Do you want to go walk on the beach later tonight?" Bennett asks me after I swim a few laps. He doesn't wait for an answer. "Remember when we were little and all we wanted was to be able to go for night walks on our own? And it seemed like a million years before we'd be able to do it?"

I nod. "It did seem like forever. But now it's here. Isn't it weird how you don't feel the passage of time when it's passing?"

"Yeah," he says. "It's like all the little days add up to a lot of time."

"Right. It's just like how it's Seagate's centennial summer." I pop under the water and then pop back up. "One hundred years is so long when you think about it, but it just passed by, one day at a time."

He squints from the late-day sun.

"I guess that's why it's so important to celebrate this big anniversary," I tell him. "Because if we don't, time just goes on and on, and no one notices that it's passed."

He hops up onto the edge of the pool and runs his hands over his wet hair. "I see what you're saying. But also, you can get so bogged down with the big things that you miss the little moments sometimes. Like how great this swim lesson is."

It feels like I've swallowed a huge clump of mashed potatoes. It was only a few minutes ago that I was counting the minutes until the lesson would end.

And before I have a chance to realize what's happening, Bennett hops back into the pool. He comes close to me, and that first-kiss conversation we had back in February pops into my head like a flashing neon sign.

But what about what he said to Calvin? How could Bennett tell Calvin to "go for it" when he wanted to kiss me a few months ago?

We lock eyes, and I can feel it—he's going to kiss me. Really kiss me. Like, on the lips.

No. No. No.

But then he flicks me on the forehead with his index finger, the way he does when he wants to zap me out of my thoughts. The moment of danger is over. I breathe a sigh of relief.

I didn't want Bennett to kiss me. But then, why did I get so upset about what he told Calvin?

*A few mornings later, we all meet at the Sea-*gate Hotel. We've started calling it the Seagate Doggie Day Camp Rainy-Day Headquarters.

We're wearing windbreakers more often than bathing suits these days. This looming grayness just isn't right.

When we do get a day at Dog Beach, I feel anxious the whole time. I want to make every moment perfect for me and my friends *and* make sure the dogs are having the best day ever. Which is impossible.

The rainy days feel hard, too. Everyone, including the dogs, seems sad and lethargic. And that makes me anxious.

But I'm most anxious about the almost-kiss with Bennett. I keep thinking about how much I didn't want it to happen. This must mean that I don't ever want to be more than friends with him. But should I tell him?

Oreo seems to have the ability to sense my anxiety. Whenever I get stressed (which is often lately) he hangs out by me, as if he wants me to know he's there.

He keeps walking up to me and sitting by my feet, like he's saying, "What's the trouble? How can I help?" His big Portuguese water dog eyes say that he has everything figured out, that he has good advice stored somewhere in his brain—like he's my dog therapist!

"Guys, come check this out," Josh calls to us from the room that used to be the library of the hotel. Micayla and Claire are in a corner of the lobby with Marilyn Monroe and Tabby, playing some kind of game where they roll a ball around and the dogs try to catch it. Bennett and Calvin are upstairs rolling up rugs and seeing if they can make more space for the dogs.

"Listen," Josh says. "This record player has been here since the 1940s. I had a specialist from the mainland come over to fix it up. And he said it's in great shape."

"Cool," I say. I sense that Josh is really excited about this, which makes me excited about it, too.

He puts on an old record. Classical music. It sounds clear and crisp and not scratchy at all. "We're gonna start using more music in our routines, so I'm pumped about this."

Right then, Lester sprints in from a corner of the room. While the music plays, Lester starts "singing." *Really* singing, with his head arched up toward the ceiling.

"Holy sssh-sugarsnaps." Josh catches himself before he swears. "That dog can sing! Yo, Juan, come over here!" he calls out.

His friend Juan and the other two Improvimaniacs run in, and Lester keeps singing along with the record.

"A whole world of possibilities just opened up," Liat says. "We have a singing dog!"

I'm happy for them. They really want to win their national competition, and now it seems that they have something the other teams won't. Maybe they can convince the Decsinis to let them borrow Lester so they can incorporate him into the routine. Lester can be their secret weapon! And the cocker spaniel seems so happy when he's singing. He's a totally different dog—alert, focused, confident.

We might never have known about Lester's hidden talent if Josh didn't play that old record. I guess the rain brought about one good thing.

Maybe everything does happen for a reason. Maybe sometimes it just takes a long time to realize what the reason is.

We hear barking coming from the other end of the room.

"Oh no!" Josh jumps up. "I was packing some boxes of stuff to send to my mom. And I forgot to put away . . ."

We turn around. We were so busy listening to Lester sing that none of us realized what was happening right behind our backs.

Tabby and Potato Salad are completely twisted up in packing tape.

It sounds like a joke: a beagle and a collie walk into some packing tape. But it's actually not funny at all.

"Oh no!" I scream. Potato Salad literally has tape wrapped around his entire body. He's straining and struggling to get out of it. And Tabby's barking, even though she only has a small piece stuck on her right paw.

But Potato Salad! Of all the dogs to get wrapped up in packing tape. Collies have long fur, and Potato Salad's is so long and beautiful.

"This isn't going to end well," Claire says, making me feel even worse about it. "I need a break."

I love Claire, but she always seems to want to leave right when we need her most. I'm not sure why. Could it be because things are already so stressful for her that she can't handle any more tension? Maybe I should be more understanding, but right now I need help.

"Okay, Mic, here's what's going to happen," I say, thinking on my feet and praying my solution will work. "You hold Potato Salad still while I very carefully try to remove the tape from his fur."

She scrunches up her face. "Ouch. This reminds me of the time I went with my sister for an eyebrow wax. Only this isn't just Potato Salad's eyebrows. This is his whole body."

"Yeah." I scrunch my face to match hers. "Major ouch."

Micayla holds Potato Salad still, even though he tries as hard as he can to break free. I take an edge of the tape that's just above his right paw and carefully pull it away. Potato

Salad emits a high-pitched yip that I've never heard before.

"It's okay, Potato Salad. We'll be done soon." I remove what tape I can while trying not to hurt him. But I need to use scissors to get the tricky spots. I snip as slowly and carefully as possible.

Finally we're done.

"Wow. That was crazy." I give Potato Salad a treat to cheer him up. I just hope his owner doesn't mind that he got a little trim! I make sure all the packing tape is out of reach and sit back down on the floor.

As stressful as that was, I'm proud of myself. We solved the problem all on our own. It makes me hopeful for many things: that we can all get through this stormy summer if we work together, that Claire and Calvin can get through the changes in their family, and that I can get through my changing feelings about Bennett and my unexpected feelings about Calvin.

It's all possible.

Claire comes back with a vanilla shake from Sundae Best. "I figured we could share this. You deserve it for handling that tape situation so calmly. It's a day for slurping," she says, quoting Josie.

"Thanks." I guess she wasn't trying to run away when the situation was difficult. She was trying to make a difficult situation better. That's important, too.

Bennett and Calvin come back from upstairs, covered in dust.

"Those windows sure needed cleaning." Bennett wipes some dirt off his forehead. "We want the dogs to be able to see outside."

I remind myself of what Claire just said. I am capable of remaining calm. If I can remain calm when a collie is wrapped up in packing tape, I can remain calm when these two boys are around.

Luckily, Potato Salad's owner isn't mad about the packing-tape incident when he comes to pick up his beautiful collie. He even thanks me for giving the dog a free haircut!

Even though I'm completely wiped out, I decide to pop into the community-planning meeting for the Seagate Centennial Summer carnival on my way home.

"You guys wanna come?" I ask my friends as we're leaving our rainy-day headquarters.

"Nah," Bennett says. "I'm exhausted."

"Same," Micayla says. "And I have plans with Gina and the crew."

"Gina and the crew" are Micayla's year-rounder friends. She doesn't see them much during the summer, but when she does, I'm reminded that things aren't the way they used to be. It's not that big of a deal, but it's still different.

"I hate carnivals," Claire adds. "I only like amusement-park rides. Rides that can be put up and taken down in an hour freak me out."

Calvin's the only one in the group who wants to come with me. But then Claire gets annoyed, because she doesn't want to go home by herself.

"Calvin, it's okay. I can go alone," I tell him as we're walking.

"Yeah, I know," he says. "But I want to help with the planning. It seems cool."

Claire walks off in a bit of a huff.

"She'll be okay," Calvin says. "I spend so much time worrying about her. I can't do it *all* the time."

I pause to think about that for a second. Calvin always seems so carefree. It makes me happy that he trusts me enough to tell me that he worries about things, too.

When we get to the planning meeting, Calvin and I take seats toward the back. As we sit quietly waiting for the meeting to start, he fiddles with a snap on the leg of his cargo shorts. Open. Closed. Open. Closed.

"So," I say. "How are things?"

He leans back in his chair so it's resting on two legs, wobbling a few times, almost falling backward.

"Come on, Calvin," I say. "Like your grandpa says, a penny for your thoughts."

"I hate when he says that," Calvin grumbles. "But okay, sure."

I nod, willing him to talk, to confide in me.

"Well, I'm thinking about how it's been over three weeks

since I spoke to my dad. And how I'm starting to lose count of how many days it's been, so I have to keep counting them again and again in my head. And then I wonder why I'm even counting at all. Does it matter how many days it's been?"

I say, "I think it matters how many days it's been because you're trying to figure out when things stopped being normal." We don't make eye contact. We're both looking down at the floor. "And you want to know how many more days it will be until things are normal again."

"Yeah," he says. "And if they ever will be."

I'm about to say that they will be normal again. In one way or another. Someday. Even if right now things seem like they'll never be. Somehow, some way, things always end up normal. Even if it's a new, lopsided kind of normal.

But that's when Mrs. Pursuit goes up to the podium. I'm almost glad for the interruption.

"Thanks so much for coming out, everyone," she says to the audience. Then she clears her throat. "I know you all have very busy Seagate summers, and I'm grateful for your help. We want to make the Centennial celebration as wonderful as it can be."

She goes down the list of all the vendors; pretty much every food establishment on Seagate is participating. There will be a stage set up for bands to perform—some from the mainland, and some Seagate bands, like our favorite, Saturday We Tennis.

"We're having the carnival rides brought in from the mainland, but we're looking for volunteers to run the booths," she says. "Also, some ideas for additional booths would be great!"

A man in the front suggests bobbing for apples. And a woman tells everyone how great she is at face-painting.

"Wonderful!" Mrs. Pursuit says. "I'm going to put a sign-up sheet over here, and you can all fill it out with the booth you'd like to run."

The meeting comes to a close, and Calvin and I try to brainstorm booth ideas.

"You know when there's a little kiddie pool, and there's, like, toy fish in it?" I ask him. "There could be a fishing booth."

We walk home and continue the discussion.

"I was at a carnival once where they had a wedding booth," he tells me.

"Yeah?"

"Yeah, it was pretty much just a person standing at a table, and kids walked up and had a five-second pretend wedding, and then they got a certificate," he explains. "Makes it seem so simple, right?"

I think I get where he's going with this, and I'm tempted to change the subject.

"They didn't have a divorce booth," he says with a jokey smile.

I nod. "I guess that would be depressing."

I don't know if that was the best response to his comment. But maybe there isn't a right one.

I need to change the tone of this conversation. And fast. So I say, "I like the wedding-booth idea. Let's do it."

"Really?" he asks.

"Yeah, let's run it together."

"Okay," he says. He sounds perkier, and I can't help but smile.

Calvin walks me home. "I'll keep thinking of other booth ideas, too," he says. "In case the other volunteers run out of ideas."

"Me too."

I fall asleep easily that night, thinking of carnival rides and cotton candy and how easy it is to hang out with Calvin.

But then a text wakes me up at one in the morning.

My heart starts pounding. I always think the worst in the middle of the night, like that one of the dogs has gone missing.

But when I see that it's from Bennett and all it says is *R u up?* my heart continues to pound, but in a different way.

I text back a simple *Yes* and wait for a reply.

But nothing comes. I stare at my phone for a good ten minutes and start to get worried all over again. What if something has happened to Bennett? But that's crazy. Nothing bad ever happens on Seagate Island. Well, except maybe a hurricane or two.

But two minutes later I hear tapping at my window. I jump up, startled. I separate my eyelet curtains and look through the glass.

Bennett is standing there.

17

"*What are you doing here?*" *I ask as soon as I'm* outside. I tried to be as quiet as possible, tiptoeing out of my bedroom, down the hallway, and out to the back porch.

"I had to talk to you," he says.

"At one in the morning?" I shriek.

"Yes. You've been totally ignoring me lately. Maybe I came on too strong with the swimming lessons? I mean, look, I know you don't like to do much exercise." He laughs.

I laugh, too, because he's right about the exercise part. It's just not my thing. "I haven't been ignoring you," I say. "I've just been really preoccupied. And when I'm preoccupied, crazy things happen, like Potato Salad and the packing tape."

He nods. "That *was* really crazy."

"Yeah, I was so scared I was going to hurt him. I thought all his fur was going to come off." I look into the distance, because the ocean seems really choppy tonight, as if a storm is brewing.

"Anyway, I couldn't sleep. I was worried something else was wrong." He looks at me, and I look away.

"Nothing else is wrong," I say. "I mean, except for the million things like Claire and Calvin's parents, and the rainy weather, and—"

He stops me midsentence. "My mom once gave me some good advice. She says never to list your problems, but to take them one at a time." He puts his feet up on the wicker ottoman. "So, where should we start?"

"What do you mean?"

"I mean, which problem should we start with?"

Maybe I said too much. For once I'm not sure I want Bennett in on my problems, since now he's one of them. I hate to think of one of my best friends as a problem, but that's how it feels. I don't know how or when my feelings for him changed, but I don't think I can tell him—I don't want to hurt him. I had wanted to get his opinion on the Claire situation, but right now it all feels too complicated.

"Let's talk more tomorrow. I'm kinda tired."

"Okay," he says, sitting up straight and looking for his fallen flip-flop. "Sounds good. Just as long as you're not mad at me."

"I could never be mad at you," I say, and then I realize that that is a complete and total lie. "Actually, I could. But I'm not mad at you right now."

He shakes his head. "You're confusing sometimes. You know that?"

"So are you," I say. I think of what he said to Calvin.

I watch Bennett as he walks down the stone path that leads all the way from the side of my house to the street in front of it. His jeans are saggy, and one of his flip-flops keeps coming off, but he doesn't seem to mind. He just goes with the flow. Maybe that's what I should do instead of avoiding him. Maybe he'll have more good advice to offer me. Maybe he'll help me make sense of things.

The next morning, I take Marilyn Monroe with me to pick up Oscar, the boxer who went missing last summer. Now that that scary incident is over and ended happily, I love remembering that night, when after hours and hours of searching for Oscar, Bennett found him. Oscar has been mostly hanging with his dog-mom, Dawn, this summer, but she thinks he's getting bored and needs some socializing. I'm happy to have him back as part of the crew.

As soon as he sees me, Oscar jumps up and puts his paws on my chest as if he's trying to give me a hug.

"Oh, Oscie," I say. "I've missed you! I can't believe it's mid-July and this is the first time I'm seeing you!"

He barks happily at that and jumps down. He goes to say hi to Marilyn Monroe, which is funny, because he's so much bigger than she is. He lies down next to her and puts his face next to hers, as if they're giving each other kisses on the cheek.

It feels good to see them together. Maybe that's what's been missing this summer—having Oscar around. It feels weird to place so much importance on one dog, but he is really fun, and he gets all the dogs playing together.

It's exactly like people. There's always one who adds so much to the group that, when they're away, something feels missing. I guess in my Seagate group, that's Bennett. When he left last summer to go on that boat trip with Calvin and his dad, everything seemed so boring. We didn't play a single game of Ping-Pong.

I'd like to say that *I'm* the one in the Seagate group who does that, but I'd be lying.

It's Bennett.

If Bennett and I were a couple, if we were more than friends, it might upset the balance of the whole group. Who likes a boyfriend-girlfriend duo in the middle of a group of friends?

It would change everything.

And then what if we broke up? What then? It would be hard on the two of us, but uncomfortable for the whole group, too. Nobody would know what to do.

I decide that Bennett and I need to stay friends. That's just the way it is.

Oscar, Marilyn Monroe, and I get to Dog
Beach, and Calvin is already there. He's by himself with
Lester. I don't remember scheduling the day that way, but
maybe there was a last-minute change. Or maybe this is Calvin's way of making an effort with Lester. He knows that the
cocker spaniel needs the extra attention.

"Where's everyone else?" I ask, trying not to sound accu-
satory.

It feels empty here with only Calvin and a few dogs. Mason
barely watches over Dog Beach these days; he's so busy with
his Italian lessons.

"Claire's not feeling well," he says. "And Bennett said he
was getting the other dogs, since he had to drop Asher off at
camp early today. I have no idea where Micayla is."

"Oh." I realize I have nothing else to add, but quickly scan my brain for something to say. "I thought of another good booth idea. I still want to run the wedding booth, though."

"Oh yeah?" He looks up at me.

"A fortune-teller booth!"

"Is there a Seagate Island fortune-teller?" he asks.

"Well, kind of. There's this woman, Callie, who works at Breakfast on the Boardwalk and reads tarot cards, and sometimes people stop in to consult her," I explain. "I'm not sure if she's right or anything, but she has some loyal customers."

"Yeah, a fortune-teller would be cool," he says.

After he lets Lester off his leash, Calvin pulls two lounges over. "Here, take a load off," he says.

I let Marilyn Monroe and Oscar free, and soon the three dogs are running into the ocean together like long-lost friends. It looks like a postcard, or maybe even an inspirational poster—a Yorkie, a boxer, and a cocker spaniel, all different sizes, colors, and personalities, frolicking in the beautiful sea together.

The poster would say something like HAPPY TOGETHER.

"Look at that," I decide to tell Calvin. "Wouldn't that make a great poster?"

"Huh?" he asks, and then he catches himself. "Oh, I spaced out there for a minute."

"I do that all the time," I say.

"Good to know I'm not alone."

"Look at the different dogs, in the sea together." I point

in front of us. "Doesn't that look like a poster you'd see in a dentist's office?"

He laughs. "Explain?"

So I tell him more, until Lester runs over to us, sopping wet. His ears are dripping onto my feet, but I don't mind at all. I'm grateful for this sunny day. And if the dogs are happy, I'm happy, too.

"It's cool we're getting to hang out," Calvin says. "I mean, we hang out all the time, but it's always in a big group and stuff."

I tense up a little and pretend a mosquito bite on my knee is really, really itchy. "Yeah."

"My sister said you're her best friend," he tells me, pretty much out of the blue.

"Oh. Um, really?" I don't know why I'm so shocked. We are close. But I've never thought of Claire as my best friend, and now I feel guilty about it.

"Yeah. I heard her talking to my mom the other day," he says. "You know how Claire is. She tries to act so tough and stuff, but the thing is, she's really not."

I turn around to make sure no one's coming. "Yeah, I know that," I say quietly. "None of us is ever all we appear to be."

"Whoa. That's deep." He laughs again.

"It's kind of true, though," I say. "Think of it this way. In New York City, people install fake walls to divide one big room and make it into separate little rooms."

"Uh-huh." Calvin's looking at me as I talk, as if he's really listening.

"And it reminds me in this weird way of what people do with their feelings. We divide them up. Sometimes we show one person one part of us, and show another person another part of us," I say. "People only see one little room, when in fact there's all this other hidden space around it." As I'm talking, I wonder if I'm making any sense whatsoever. But it still feels good to say it. It's been in my head for so long, it's a relief to tell someone.

"I think you're right," he says.

"You do?"

"Yeah, I mean, like, you guys don't know everything about me," he explains. "I'm a different way around my friends at school. And I'm different around my dad than I am around my mom. That kind of thing."

"So you get what I'm saying?" I ask.

"Totally." He smiles.

I think that's the most important thing in a friend—to know that he or she understands you.

Right then, Micayla and Bennett arrive with the rest of the dogs, and in a way I'm sad to end our conversation.

"What's up?" Micayla asks when all the dogs have settled down and are enjoying their morning snack with the boys.

"Claire's sick," I tell her. "Calvin told me."

"Oh. Anything else?"

"*Nuh*-thing," I say, sounding more defensive than I'd planned. But it seems as if Micayla knows there's something I'm not telling her.

"Sheesh, okay!" She laughs. "Guess you woke up on the wrong side of the bed."

"No, no," I say, defending myself. "I'm fine. I just don't have much else to share at the moment." I stare off at the sea, happy to be alone with my thoughts. All I can think about is that conversation with Calvin.

"Remy, your head is in the clouds again today," Micayla says. "I can tell. So here's something to zap you back to earth."

"What?"

"You know how everyone keeps saying this is gonna be a bad hurricane season?"

I nod. Well, that was quick. She completely zapped me out of my happy thoughts.

"What if we have to evacuate?" she asks me.

"Come on. Don't think about that," I plead. "There's always hurricane talk, and besides, we can't know in advance. We don't need to worry about it now."

"Well, I do worry about it," she says. "I have no idea where we'll go if we have to evacuate. It didn't really occur to me until yesterday, when I overheard my parents talking about it in a joking way while they were making dinner. We don't have our New Jersey house anymore. My grandma moved into an assisted-living place. We'll be homeless!"

"Mic, come on. They were joking. You said so yourself." I try to rein her in. "Plus, your parents have a billion friends. Worse comes to worst, you'll move in with us in New York."

"Come on. Really?" She glares.

"Yes, of course. You can sleep on my top bunk."

She nods. "Okay, thanks. Good backup plan. But, seriously! I was just getting used to being a year-rounder."

"I know."

I guess that's something about life that's hard to understand. Just when you get used to something, it can change.

19

I wake up covered in sweat, my heart thumping.
I was dreaming that I was trapped underground on the sub-
way between two stops for hours and hours. It's a recurring
dream I have whenever I'm worried about something. And
I hate it. Truthfully, I've only been stuck on the train a few
times, and usually not for that long. But in my nightmare,
we're stranded in the pitch-darkness, and people start
screaming, and no one can get off the train.

Downstairs, my parents are drinking lattes from the new
coffee place, Seagate Sips. They usually make their own
coffee, but they love morning walks, and they can't resist
supporting a local business.

"If we have to evacuate Seagate, the Walcotts are coming
with us," I declare, as though it's a law and there's absolutely
no debating it.

"Um, well, evacuating is really a worst-case scenario if that low-pressure system making its way up from the south actually turns into a hurricane and hits us; no one has said anything about that yet," Dad replies. "But we'd certainly help them in any way we could." He finishes his latte. "I'm not sure they'd want to come back to Manhattan and live in such a small space with us, though."

"There's no other choice!" I cry. "They have nowhere else to go. They sold their New Jersey house." I go on and on about Micayla's grandma in assisted living and how they'll be homeless if they have to leave the island. "They'll have to go back to St. Lucia. And then I'll never see my best friend again."

"Remy, you're getting way ahead of yourself," Mom says in her please-calm-down tone. She seems to use this tone more and more lately.

"Yeah, but everyone keeps saying how it's gonna be a bad hurricane season," I remind them.

With a sigh my mom says, "It will be okay. Just relax."

If I had a dollar for every time someone told me to "just relax," I'd be able to buy a new apartment for myself in Manhattan.

I grab Marilyn Monroe and we walk over to check on Claire. She hasn't responded to my calls or texts, and I'm worried that she's really sick. After that, Mari and I will go get Lester, since he seems to have much better days when I pick him up.

I ring the doorbell at Mr. Brookfield's house, and he comes to the door a few minutes later.

"Hello, Remy," he says in his trying-to-be-cheerful tone. Then he screams his famous scream. *"Aaaaheeeeooww-wwww!"*

I try to mimic it, but my effort can't compare.

"I wanted to check on Claire," I tell him.

"She's upstairs. You can go on up."

I wonder if Calvin's home, too, or if he's already on his way to Dog Beach. I seem to be thinking a lot about him these days.

"Claire?" I say softly through the closed door to her room. Nothing.

"Claire? Are you okay?"

Marilyn Monroe's little Yorkie ears perk up, and she looks up at me as if she's concerned, as if she has something to tell me.

"What do you want, Remy?" Claire asks.

Not the greeting I had hoped for, but that's okay. "May I come in?"

"Sure."

I walk in and find Claire lying in bed, under her covers, a pillow over her head.

I sit down on the very edge of the mattress. "I came to check on you."

She doesn't respond.

"I was thinking about what you said. About how you were

once a family." I pause. "And you still are. Maybe you're a little broken now. But, like, here's the thing I was thinking about. My aunt Evelyn made a quilt for me before I was even born. Patchwork. It had all these beautiful pastel squares, some with patterns, some solid. Anyway, I slept with it every night. And little by little, it started to tear. My mom tried to sew it, but she's not the best sewer, and eventually a piece of it completely came off. I was four then, and I was all upset. I said I didn't want it anymore, but deep down, I did. After I was done being mad, I realized that the quilt was still good. And it had some advantages—like, when I slept away from home, at my grandparents' house in Connecticut, or at my aunt and uncle's in Baltimore, I could easily bring the little piece with me. Both parts of the quilt were special in their own way."

Claire throws the pillow to the edge of her bed. I think she was trying to hit me, but she missed.

She sits up and glares at me. "Remy. That's the dumbest thing I've ever heard."

I guess it was kind of dumb. But I stand by it. "A broken thing can still be a happy thing. That's all I'm saying."

"I understand," she says, not overly thrilled.

"Well, get up. We need you at doggie day camp."

"It's pouring out," Claire reminds me.

"I know. Rainy-day headquarters."

Claire takes too long to get ready, but we're finally out the door and on our way to get Lester.

"Thanks for picking him up," his owner-dad says. "The

kids are driving him crazy. We think maybe he's scared of loud noises. We're looking into some kind of dog psychiatrist for him when we get back from Seagate."

"I see." Scared of loud noises? I'm not sure. He liked that record Josh put on, and it was pretty loud. Still, I guess a dog psychiatrist is worth a try. "Well, it's no problem for me to pick him up. I think it helps him."

Claire, Marilyn Monroe, Lester, and I hustle as fast as we can over to the hotel.

We find the rest of the crew inside. The Improvimaniacs are practicing with Tabby, Potato Salad, Oreo, and Ritzy. Some kind of doggie game show. Bennett and Calvin are in the back of the room, fully cracking up. Literally falling on the floor in laughter.

It's funny, but not *that* funny.

Micayla's on the window seat, getting the dogs' morning treats together.

"I have to talk to you," I whisper to her when I know Claire's distracted. "Remember when you said Calvin liked me? And I kind of ignored it?"

She nods.

"He's been talking to me more and more. I think he *does* like me."

"Obviously." She arches an eyebrow.

"But what am I going to do?" I whisper. "I think I like him, too. What about Bennett? I thought I liked him. But I don't anymore."

"I think this is what's commonly known as a love triangle," Micayla jokes, but I wish she'd realize this isn't a joking matter. "You have to tell Claire," she says. "It could be really awkward for her."

I nod. "What about Bennett?"

"You should tell him, too," she says.

"But remember when you said that Bennett told Calvin that he should just go for it?" I whisper and look around, nervous someone will overhear or come up behind me when I'm not paying attention. My stomach twists around itself in a spiral like one of those giant, colorful lollipops.

"Yeah, but he might have just been saying that to be nice—and to not give away his own feelings. You know guys," Micayla says. "But, Remy, you're freaking out. Let's talk later."

I peek out the window and see a glimmer of sun coming from the north. "Looks like the weather is clearing up. We can get the dogs outside soon." I've only been here a few minutes, and I'm grateful we have a rainy-day headquarters, but I'm starting to feel claustrophobic.

"Lester! Come back! Lester," Bennett yells as he runs through the lobby, out the open door, and onto the sidewalk. The screen door slams behind him.

Things with Lester haven't improved at all; in fact, I'm pretty sure they've gotten worse. He always seems to be running away every chance he gets. At first I thought it had to do with Ritzy, and then maybe loud noises, as his owner-dad said, but now I'm not sure. He runs away when things are quiet, too. I'm beginning to think the dog psychiatrist is the only way we'll ever really find out what's troubling him.

"Any idea where Lester might be running to?" Calvin asks.

"Mic, Claire, stay here with the dogs, okay?" I say. "Calvin, come with me. You run faster than I do. We need to go look for him."

Micayla groans. "Fine."

Calvin and I run as fast we can to catch up to Bennett, who's running super fast to try to find Lester.

"Anyone see a cocker spaniel run by?" I ask people as we pass.

They shrug, offer worried expressions, and tell us they'll let us know if they see him.

Finally, after checking Dog Beach, Daisy's, and Mornings, we find him.

"I guess he wants to learn how to read," Bennett offers.

Lester is curled up in the sandpile under the bench outside Novel Ideas.

"Lester." I bend down and scoop him out.

"He's a big fan of the store," Mr. Aprone says, popping his head out the door. "He likes biographies."

I can't tell if he's joking or not, so I smile and pet Lester's head. I notice how relaxing it is in the store, with beautiful classical music playing through the aisles of books. "He comes prepared, you should know. Like he's planning to be here a while. He usually has half of someone's breakfast sandwich in his mouth." Mr. Aprone laughs. "You're prepared for anything, Lester. Aren't you?"

I sigh, exasperated. "Thanks, Mr. Aprone. See you soon."

As we're walking back to headquarters, I keep thinking about the whole concept of being prepared. In a way, it's all we can do. And being prepared can make you feel calmer. But on the other hand, how do you decide what to prepare for when there are so many things that can go wrong?

I expected everything to be smooth and easy this summer. But it's not. The weather's weird, Claire is sad, and I seem to be getting squeezed into a corner of what Micayla called a love triangle.

It's like this mint-green dress I have—no matter how well it's ironed, the minute I put it on, it looks wrinkled, as if I'd just picked it out of a pile of dirty laundry on my floor. It almost feels pointless to iron it, but Mom does it anyway.

This summer feels like that dress. The season started out all ironed and perfect, but now it's more wrinkled than it's ever been before.

The rain. Claire and Calvin's family. My feelings about Bennett and Calvin. Wrinkle, wrinkle, wrinkle.

"*Swim lesson?*" *Bennett asks me. We've had a* short string of sunny days, and we're all walking home together after dropping the dogs off at their houses.

I have to tell him. This is the time. I feel as if I'm carrying a backpack of bricks.

"Sure," I say, and Bennett looks a little shocked. He expected me to say no after I had canceled so many times. Bennett tells me he'll meet me at my house in fifteen minutes. He has to run home and change.

"Wait, so what's happening now?" Claire whispers to me as we're walking.

"Bennett's giving me swimming lessons," I say. "Or trying to. I mean, it's barely been swimming weather. But I think I may want to try out for the team."

She laughs a little meanly at the idea of me on a swim

team. Then she asks, "You and Bennett, alone, in your pool?"

"Yeah." I shrug. "Why not? We've been alone in a pool together a million times." I decide to play it cool and act carefree, just like Calvin would do. I can't tell Claire what I'm about to tell Bennett. I need to tell Bennett first. That's one thing I know for sure.

"How are you doing?" I ask her. I genuinely want to know, but I also want to take a break from my own worries.

"Fine." Claire shrugs. "Why?"

"I mean, really, how are you doing?" I look at her, but she continues to stare at the sidewalk. "We haven't really talked since the day I told you about Aunt Evelyn's quilt."

"Oh yeah, everything is still terrible," she says. "I wake up every day thinking it'll be better. But it's not. It's like that conveyor belt at the airport that goes around and around and around with your luggage."

"How so?" I ask.

"It's just an endless loop of the same bad stuff. Now my parents are fighting about custody of Calvin and me. But it's such a joke, because my dad is always traveling. And my mom has late meetings all the time. So it'll be bad either way."

Sometimes all it takes is hearing someone else's problems to realize that your problems aren't actually problems at all.

"That sounds so terrible," I say, afraid that I sound as if I'm reading from a script.

"It *is* terrible." Claire looks at me finally. "It's not fair. My parents *chose* to get married, and they *chose* to have Calvin and me. And now they're *choosing* to get a divorce. Why don't Calvin and I get any choices in the matter?"

I've never thought about it like that, and it makes me sad. Claire must feel even less in control of her life than I do!

Claire continues, kicking a pebble on the path as we walk. "And they're always saying how it's not our fault and they still love us. But they're still divorcing. It's not like their love for us is making them stay together. Now I have to be the girl with the divorced parents." She wipes a tear away. "I don't want to be that girl."

I nod. I know the best thing I can do right now is listen.

"Kids have no rights, and we have no say," she tells me, as if she's making a protest speech in front of hundreds of people. "It doesn't matter what we think or what we want. Adults do what they want to do."

"You're right. It totally stinks. And it's totally unfair," I say.

"But what can I do?" She ties her hair back in a ponytail. She's getting sweaty and fired up talking about this. "Nothing."

"You could start a support group," I suggest. The words are out of my mouth before I realize how stupid they sound.

"Yeah?" Claire asks. I can't tell if she's about to be sarcastic or if she wants to hear more. That's the issue with Claire—sometimes she's very hard to read. Even for me.

I continue. "Yeah, like, so many kids go through this, and they probably all feel powerless and helpless and that everything is so unfair. Because it is," I tell her. "And they probably need to talk about it, too. You know, get their frustrations out."

Claire is quiet.

"I mean, do you feel better talking to me about it?" I ask her.

She waits a second before replying. "I think so. I mean, yes. I do."

"So that's a start," I tell her. "Everyone needs to vent and get things off their chest. Sometimes even complaining helps."

"You think so?" Claire giggles in her charming Claire way, and things feel instantly better.

"Definitely. And not everyone has an amazing friend like me to complain to!" I look at her and see that she's smiling and her shoulders don't seem so hunched. Maybe I've helped. Oh, please, please, let me have helped.

"I could call it the complainers club," she says. "And people could complain about whatever they wanted."

"Exactly." She's listening to me. Claire's actually listening to me. I've been trying so hard to figure out a way to help, but my dad was right. Listening and being there for her was the best way.

"You could run the Kids Complainers Club!" I pat her on the arm. "It has a great ring to it. Doesn't it?"

"Will you join my complainers club? Even though you don't have divorced parents? It can be for anyone who wants to complain about anything." She laughs a little bit, as if she can't really take it seriously yet. I'll admit, it does sound a little funny.

"I'd love to, *dahling*," I say in a fake British accent for no reason at all.

"Very well, *dahling*," Claire mimics.

We walk hand in hand for a minute before Claire says, "You need to get home for your swimming lesson. We passed your house five minutes ago."

I look around and realize she's right. I was so engrossed in our conversation that I totally forgot where I was and where I was going.

"Good luck," she says. "I hope you learn to swim."

"Ha-ha."

As I walk alone to my house, I can't help but smile. Because even though Claire is going through a bad time right now, I was able to help her a little bit. And that makes me feel happy. Claire even seemed happier, too.

Little bits of happiness are better than no happiness at all.

Bennett is waiting for me by the pool when I get home.

"Took you long enough," he groans.

I look around, because I'm not sure if my parents are home or not.

It seems he can read my mind. "Your parents went to Frederick's Fish to get tuna steaks to grill tonight," he tells me. "I'm staying for dinner."

"Okay, then." I laugh.

It seems Bennett knows more about what's going on around here than I do. Maybe I shouldn't tell him how I feel if he's staying for dinner. My parents are probably buying a tuna steak for him as we speak. I think of a million more reasons why now is definitely not the time to tell him.

"So, let's see your strokes," he says, leaning back in a

lounge chair, his hands behind his head. He's wearing a baggy blue bathing suit and a Seagate Island Pizzeria T-shirt. He looks as if he has no intention of getting into the pool. I can't decide if I want him to or not.

"Strokes?" I ask. "I basically do the doggie paddle."

"Well, you can't join a swim team on the doggie paddle, babe," he says, and I crack up.

"Babe?" Since when does he call me *babe*?

Bennett laughs at himself, and I shake my head at him.

"I guess I can attempt the crawl. Tell me what you think."

I walk over to the other side of the pool, pull off my cover-up, and jump in. Once I'm in the water, I realize that I am not embarrassed for Bennett to see me in my swimsuit anymore.

"The key to a good crawl is making sure you reach out your arms as far as you can," he tells me. "Like you're trying to reach and scoop something out of the water."

I start at the end of the pool near the diving board and try to do my most perfect crawl stroke to the other side. I stretch out my arms all the way and turn my head from side to side. As I'm swimming, I'm not thinking about anything else, only breathing and kicking and moving my arms. For a second I almost forget that Bennett's watching.

But then I reach the other side and pop my head out of the water. And there's Bennett, standing an inch away from me, his toes on the edge of the pool.

"Good job," he says. "But it needs some work." He sits down and dangles his legs in the water. "You need to scoop your hands a little more, not slap them down," he tells me. "It'll make the whole thing smoother and more graceful."

I nod. I don't know if he's going to get into the pool or stay there and give me more advice on how to improve my stroke.

As always, it's the not knowing that's hard.

I tie my chlorine-y hair into a ponytail, and Bennett plops into the water and sinks to the bottom of the pool.

"Here, watch me," he says when he pops back up.

And then he takes off in a fast crawl—so fast, I bet he could train for the Olympics.

"See how I turn my face?" he asks when he gets back to me. "You only need to turn it to the side a little, not lift up your whole head. I'm going to be a tough coach. Because I know you can do it."

I can't help it. I burst out laughing. Bennett is suddenly Mr. Tough Swim Coach! It's too much.

"Hey!" He splashes me as hard as he can. "I'm only trying to help."

"Fine. I'm sorry." I'm still laughing on the inside, but I control my giggles. "Thanks for your help."

We go over the crawl a few more times, and then he says he wants to move on to the sidestroke.

"The crawl is enough for today," I tell him. "I need to master that one first."

He nods. "Fair enough. Want to see my double flip off the diving board?"

"Of course I do."

And just like that, things feel normal again. As if nothing has changed between us.

I want to tell him that he's still my best friend, but my dad comes outside and starts grilling, and my mom is pouring us strawberry lemonade.

Everything feels perfect again. I don't want to mess it up.

Lester continues to run away every chance he gets. At this point, I'm pretty sure it's a game to him. I see a little twinkle in his eye when he does it.

"Lester," I say, pulling him to the side, away from the other dogs. I feel like I'm a teacher and he's a student. I try to speak in a calm voice. "Let's have a heart-to-heart."

Maybe I'll be a dog psychiatrist myself one day.

I get him to calm down, and we sit next to each other, his paw on my knee. "You can't run away like that." I look into his big, droopy, cocker spaniel eyes. "Don't you understand that it's dangerous?"

He stares at me. I rub his sandy-colored fur.

"Lester, please, just give me some kind of signal that you understand me." I wait for a bark or a raised ear or even a tail wag. But nothing. And then he takes off again, sprinting toward the white fence at the edge of Dog Beach.

"Lester!" I yell, and I run after him.

I catch up to him and put him on his leash; he's left me no other choice.

He spends the rest of the day with his leash tied to one of the legs of my lounge chair.

As he lies there in the sun, the other dogs periodically come to check on him. Ritzy, especially. And his ears perk up whenever she comes close.

Maybe that's why he was running away? Because he wanted to see if I'd come after him and find a way to keep him close by? It seems strange, but I think we all get this way on occasion.

Sometimes we want to run away to see if people will come rescue us.

I think about Lester running to Novel Ideas and curling up under that bench, with Mr. Aprone's soft music wafting through the air. Something must comfort him as he sits there and watches the people go in and out of the store. Something makes him feel safe, as if he's not so alone.

That's how I feel about Seagate. I feel safe here. Relaxed. The world can feel so big and scary sometimes. We all need a place where everything feels okay.

"So, did you tell Bennett?" Micayla asks me while the Improvimaniacs are practicing with the dogs. It's pretty nice having them around. The dogs love them, and it means we get a little break from tending to them. It's a win-win for everyone.

"Not yet." I explain the swim lesson and the tuna steaks for dinner.

"You're chickening out," Mic says.

"Am not."

"Yes, you are. Just do it. It'll be a huge relief."

I know she's right. But it's weird that Micayla seems so concerned about this. Almost too concerned.

"I'll do it. Okay? Sheesh."

Micayla and I continue this almost-fight for a few seconds, and then we both start laughing. The kind of laughing where we can't stop, where our stomachs hurt, where a little bit of spit comes out of our mouths and lands on our shirts. Gross but true.

"What's so funny?" Calvin asks. "Did you guys see what we just did?"

We shake our heads.

"We had a pretend wedding for Tabby and Oreo. Josh asked us to throw out random words for the Improvimani-acs to play off of for the next skit. So I threw out *divorce*, and they started with Tabby and Oreo having a fight, but then it turned into a flashback of their wedding." He starts laughing after he says it, but then his eyes turn sad; it's as if halfway through he realized what he was saying. As if it took his heart a few seconds to catch up to what his brain was thinking.

I laugh, too. But it's too late. I know it is. I see Calvin's sad eyes.

"Anyway, it was funny," he says softly and quickly, as if he wants to end this conversation before it really has a chance to get started.

"Sounds like it," I say. I go to put a hand on his shoulder, but I pull away before it lands there. I know that Calvin wants me to act happy, not concerned. I guess that's what makes *him* feel safe—staying in a happy place. So, for that moment, I do.

"Hey, Remy." **Mrs. Pursuit comes over to my** table at Daisy's.

Marilyn Monroe and I are having breakfast before we meet the others at the hotel.

It may be rainy again, and our moods may be dampened, but that only means we need Daisy's even more.

"Hi." I look up from my cinnamon-roll pancakes.

"Great turnout at the meeting the other day, huh?" She smiles. "I was very pleased. And I'm excited that you want to help."

I stare at my pancakes. Would it be rude to continue eating while she talks? My food is getting cold. And soggy. I hate soggy pancakes.

"Would you like to sit down?" I ask her.

"No, no, that's okay." I take that to mean it's fine for me to eat another bite. "I have a stack of fliers here, advertising the carnival and looking for people to run booths."

I nod. I know it's rude to talk with food in my mouth.

She smiles and finally decides to sit down. "So, any chance you could hand out these fliers to people while you're out and about today?"

I look at the window. Maybe she doesn't realize that it's raining. Maybe she's not worried that her fliers will get wet.

"Sure," I say when I'm done chewing. "No problem."

On my way to headquarters, I hand some fliers out, and people seem excited about the carnival. I tack some up on the local bulletin boards, too.

Maybe it's the cinnamon-roll pancakes, or maybe it's that Mrs. Pursuit asked for my help, but I'm energized. The rain can't ruin this summer on Seagate! Claire seems happier lately, and right this moment, everything feels as if it's going to be okay.

Marilyn Monroe practically skips into the old Seagate Hotel.

But overhearing a conversation stops me when I'm half-way inside.

"She likes you," I hear Micayla say.

"She does?" Calvin asks.

Uh-oh. I know what they're talking about. I know *who* they're talking about.

"I wanted you to know. Remy's pretty shy about saying

what's on her mind," Micayla says. "And she's kind of drag-
ging her feet."

Micayla's shy about saying stuff, too. I can't believe she's
doing this!

"Well, uh, thanks for letting me know." Calvin's voice gets
quieter.

I know what that means. Bennett must be nearby.

I hear a loud belch and then, "Yo, my people!" It's Bennett,
of course. "Are you guys coming to help?" he asks. "The dogs
are bored. And frankly, so am I!"

"We're coming. We're coming," Micayla groans.

"I feel bad for Bennett," she says quietly to Calvin.

I can't see her face. Or Calvin's. But I can't believe she'd
talk to Calvin about this. I feel as if I can never trust her
again.

For a few days, I ignore the conversation I overheard, because I don't know what to do about it. Why would Micayla talk to Calvin behind my back?

The Centennial Summer celebration is in a few days, and it's way more fun to focus on that.

So many people signed up to perform that Mrs. Pursuit wants to have a run-through at the stadium to make sure everything goes smoothly. And she asked if I could be around to help out. We got special permission to bring the dogs there, as long as we promise to clean up any messes. But I know that our dogs won't cause any problems.

The days in our rainy-day headquarters were getting pretty boring for them, and since watching people perform is fun for people, I figure it's gotta be fun for dogs, too. But at this point, what they really need is a change of pace.

"Guys, you need to behave," I tell the dogs. They're all sitting in a row like perfect little angels. I know it won't last, though. They're behaving now because I gave them treats as soon as we arrived. "We won't be here all day. Just the morning. Okay?"

I wait for responses.

Marilyn Monroe and Tabby bark as if they've understood, but the rest of them just stare at me with their big eyes, their tongues hanging out. It's hot today, for a change, and I don't think they're quite used to it.

The performers arrive, and I think they're a little shocked to see so many dogs and kids but so few adults.

"We're, um, here for the run-through," an older guy tells me, confused, probably thinking he's in the wrong place. His son is with him. I think they're new to Seagate this summer. "We're a father-son juggling duo."

"Great." I smile. "Just take a seat on the benches over there."

He gives me a quizzical look.

"Mrs. Pursuit is running late, so I offered to help get things started." She's pretty much always running late.

"Got it," he says.

When all the performers are there, and the dogs are quiet (for the moment), I stand up and make an announcement. "Thank you all for coming. Mrs. Pursuit just wanted to do a quick run-through so everyone knows the order and how much time they have onstage."

Lester tries to run away, but Bennett grabs him and ties his leash to one of the stadium columns.

"Okay, Mari, keep an eye on everyone," I whisper into her ear, and she pops up to lick my cheek. I've designated her to be the babysitter of the bunch. I'm not sure how she feels about it and not sure it will work, but these things are always worth a try.

"First up, we have Larry Park," I say. "It says here you're a classical pianist."

Uh-oh. I should have looked more closely at this list. There's only one piano on Seagate, and it's in the senior center on the other end of the island. Maybe someone can go and get it before the carnival, but it's too late now.

I'm about to apologize for this when I see Larry Park carrying a portable keyboard to the front.

"I came prepared," he says, and I relax. "It's unusual, but I consider myself a classical *keyboardist*. I rarely play on a regular piano anymore."

"That's . . . great," I say, perplexed but relieved.

He continues. "I live in a tiny studio apartment in Brooklyn most of the year, and I'm here in the summer. No room for a real piano. Life is all about making do with what you have."

I think about how true this is, and it makes me smile. I need to remember that, when things seem impossible, there's always a way to make do with what you have.

Larry sets up his keyboard and then tells everyone that he'll be playing a Bach Invention in C-sharp major.

The music is upbeat and happy, and I wish he could play for the rest of the day. He's really talented.

Halfway through, though, things start to get crazy. Not with Larry Park or his music.

It's Lester.

The cocker spaniel starts singing along with the keyboard! I try to quiet him down, but Lester won't stop singing. Not barking or howling, but singing. He sits up really tall and arches his neck and holds his muzzle up toward the sky. And then he sings. Really sings. As if he's part of Larry's performance. It almost seems as though Larry Park is *Lester's* accompanist.

"Ssshhh, Lester," I hear Micayla whisper. The cocker spaniel looks at her for a second, but he doesn't stop. He doesn't even seem embarrassed. And, yes, dogs can get embarrassed. I've seen it before.

But Lester is a natural performer.

Larry keeps playing, and thankfully he's a good sport about it. He even seems to be enjoying Lester's performance.

When he's done, Larry says, "I'd like to add that dog to my routine."

We all laugh.

"I'm not kidding." He smiles. "I think we'd work well together."

"Um, okay, well, thanks so much. We can certainly put you in touch with his owner."

Larry nods. "Sounds great."

It seems as if Lester has been waiting all summer for Larry Park, for this moment and this music.

A few singers follow Larry. A drummer. An acoustic guitarist who plays a Beatles medley. And our favorite Seagate band, Saturday We Tennis, complete with a bass and cello. But nothing gets Lester to sing like Larry Park's classical music.

Obviously Lester's very sophisticated.

The more I think about it, the more I realize that I can relate to Lester and his mad dashes for freedom. Maybe I've been running away, too. I've been running away from how I really feel about Calvin. And I've been running away from telling Bennett how I feel about staying just friends.

Maybe we're all running away from something. Maybe some things are just too complicated to focus on.

The rest of the group works overtime taking care of the dogs while I keep track of how much time everyone needs for his or her act.

Finally it's the Improvimaniacs' turn. And even though I've seen them practicing, I'm excited to see them on an actual stage.

Since the doggie day care staff are the only ones left (most of the performers had other places to be), we get to throw out words to help the guys get started with their improv act. Calvin says, "Dental floss," and they end up doing a whole routine about a crazy dentist who uses chocolate instead of toothpaste.

We all crack up.

It's pretty amazing that Josh and the Improvimaniacs can do such funny stuff with so little planning. Actually, there's no planning at all. Their whole act is based on surprise, on *not* knowing what to expect. How do they do it?

We're walking the dogs home when I realize what I've needed to understand all along: this is a summer of surprises. We've all been facing the unexpected or trying to prepare for things you can't really prepare for. But sometimes you just have to go with the flow and work with what comes your way—just like Josh's improv group.

"You seem happy," Calvin says, catching up to me. I was alone with Marilyn Monroe, Tabby, Potato Salad, and Lester and didn't even realize it. Bennett and Micayla left to take Rascal home, and we are all going to meet at Sundae Best afterward.

"I *am* happy," I say. "I realized something that's really, really obvious, but for some reason, I never thought of it before."

"What is it? That it's really delicious to dip your fries in mayonnaise?"

"Gross!" I laugh. "No, I realized that unexpected things can be good, even fun. I spend my whole life planning and wanting everything to stay the same, but sometimes it's good when things surprise you."

He looks at me. "You sound like my grandfather. What do you mean, your 'whole life'? You're twelve, Remy, not eighty-five."

"Oh, never mind," I say, a little embarrassed.

He elbows me. "Come on, Rem. I'm just teasing you."

I look at him for a second. I can't run away from this any-more. I know he likes me. And he knows I like him.

"Listen, Calvin," I begin.

"I'm listening." He laughs.

"I . . ." What was I thinking? I can't tell him yet. I haven't told Bennett. I haven't told Claire.

"Yeah?" he asks.

"Never mind," I mumble again. "I forgot what I was going to say."

25

"Calvin keeps asking me what's going on," Micayla tells me. We're on my back porch, eating take-out sandwiches from Frederick's Fish. Our moms have book club tonight, and our dads are at a Seagate Community Council meeting. We decided to have an old-fashioned sleepover, just the two of us. Claire's mom is here this week anyway, so I don't feel too bad about leaving her out. But I'm still a little uncomfortable with Micayla after overhearing her talk to Calvin. I feel hurt that she went behind my back.

"What do you mean?" I ask, even though I know what she means.

She rolls her eyes. She knows me too well. "He wants to know if I've told you he likes you. And he wants to know if you think Bennett will be mad, and if Claire will think it's weird. And a million other things."

I laugh. "Why is he asking you for all these answers?"

"Because I can predict the future. Micayla Walcott, fortune-teller. That's what everyone says."

"That's true. You should run the fortune-teller booth at the Centennial carnival."

"That sounds like a great idea!" she says.

I throw away the wrapper from my fish sandwich and come back to my Adirondack chair. "I need to talk to you about something."

"What?"

"I overheard you talking to Calvin the other day," I announce.

She's quiet.

"Why'd you do that?" I ask softly. "I thought I could trust you."

She bites the inside of her cheek. "I don't know why I did it, exactly."

"Really?" Somehow I don't believe her.

She inches forward on her Adirondack chair. "I was helping you," she explains. "I was moving things along."

"I can handle things when I'm ready," I say defensively.

"But you never are. You just wait and wait and think and think." She looks away. "And Bennett's waiting around, all in love with you. And now Calvin likes you, too. And you're just ignoring the whole thing." She pauses. "It's kind of rude to both of them."

"Bennett's not in love with me," I say under my breath.

"Yes he is, Remy," she says.

"Well, I need to talk to him. And then I need to talk to Claire." Saying all this out loud feels overwhelming. I swallow hard. "And then I'll talk to Calvin. Okay?"

"Fine. Can we go in the pool now?"

I nod. We grab towels out of the basket by the door and spread them out on lounges.

"So, what's the latest with you and Mason?" I ask after a few seconds of awkward silence in the pool.

"Oh, we're done," she says. "I ended things last week."

I flip over in the pool and pop back up, waiting for her to say more. "You didn't tell me."

"I didn't tell you because I didn't think you'd care. You're so focused on your own stuff, you haven't asked anything about me and Mason for weeks."

Her words sting, and I feel like a bad friend. I want to be a good friend more than anything. "That's not true. You know I'm always here for you."

She rolls her eyes at me again and then continues talking about Mason. "I mean, he was nice, but I felt like he was practically a study partner, always trying so hard to say interesting stuff. It felt like I was going out with an encyclopedia."

"Really?"

"He'd just spew out random facts and information, and I never knew how to respond. And he'd never ask me about myself," she tells me. "The whole thing got really tiring. Plus, whenever he'd try to hold my hand, his hands were always so sweaty."

"It *is* summer, Mic." I pull over the double raft and hop up, urging her to do the same so we can float around together. "People sweat." I feel the need to defend Mason, maybe because now I'm afraid that she thinks we're both selfish.

"Thanks. I know that," she tells me, inching a little away from me on the raft. "There's also something else I've been waiting to tell you."

"What is it?"

"I'm scared to say it."

My body tightens up. "Just say it," I groan, even though I know it's just as hard for Micayla to get things off her chest as it is for me.

She sits up and holds her forehead. "You're not the only one who likes—I mean, *liked*—Bennett."

I look at her. Is she saying what I think she's saying?

"Wait," I say. "*You* like Bennett? No!"

"Yes."

Just when I thought I was learning to accept the unexpected, this surprise feels like a tree branch falling on my head.

"Why do you care?" she asks, hopping off the raft. She hoists herself up onto the edge of the pool. "You don't like him."

I stay on the raft, alone. It feels a little funny, but I'm too shocked to move.

"I know," I say under my breath, but a little part of me still doesn't want Micayla to like Bennett. And another little part doesn't want Bennett to like her.

And maybe that makes me an even worse friend.

26

I thought that Micayla and I would stay up all night discussing the Bennett thing, but we didn't. My mom came home from book club, and she brought us home Sundae Best ice cream, and we appreciated the distraction.

We didn't stay up late talking at all. We went straight to bed. Now it's been three days, and we still haven't discussed our situation. I keep waiting for her to bring it up, but she doesn't. And I keep thinking I should bring it up, but I chicken out every time.

I'm running away from my problems again, just like Lester.

I try to watch Micayla and Bennett when they're together, and everything seems about the same, Bennett cracking jokes, Micayla laughing. Micayla telling some funny story about her sister's Halloween costume, and Bennett asking questions, as if he's more interested in her story than anything else in the world.

But that's how Bennett is with everybody. That's what makes him unique. He asks you questions and treats you like you're the only person in the world. He makes the world feel calm and at ease. That's why he's such a good friend.

When we're all together, I spend a lot of time wondering if he knows about Micayla. And I wonder if he knows how I feel about Calvin.

I've been ignoring my problems and questions all summer, glancing at them warily from time to time, the way I do the sky, seeking storm clouds, but I can't ignore them anymore.

Bennett and I are sitting at the table by my pool after a swim lesson. We're eating cut-up strawberries and bananas, discussing how I can better my backstroke. And that's when it happens.

Without thinking, I ask, "What do you think of Micayla?"

He swallows a strawberry. "What d'you mean?"

I turn away, pretending I hear something off in the distance. "Never mind. So, how do I get my elbows higher out of the water when I'm swimming the crawl? It seems easy when I think about it, but then when I get into the pool, my arms feel so heavy." I sip my lemonade. "I mean, one arm goes the right way, and the other feels totally out to the side."

He gives me a funny look. "What were you saying about Micayla?"

"Oh, nothing." I look away again. I pray for my mom to

come outside, or my phone to buzz, or anything. Even a rain-storm would be helpful at this moment.

"Fine. I have a question for you," he says, and I expect him to ask something doofy about who has more nose hair, Mr. Brookfield or Potato Salad's owner.

"What do *you* think about *Calvin*?"

I force myself to keep a straight face and act as if all this isn't a big deal. As if I have no idea what he's talking about.

"He's a nice kid. I dunno. Why?"

"Remy." He glares.

"Bennett." I meet his glare and give one right back.

"I'm not going to tell you what I think about Micayla until you tell me what you think about Calvin."

"I guess we won't be talking much, then," I say, picking a strawberry out of the bowl. "Because there's nothing to tell."

"Fine."

"Fine."

But I know I need to say it. Now is the time. Enough is enough.

We stare at each other for a few seconds, and finally I take a big breath and say, "I've actually been meaning to talk to you about that."

He nods.

"The truth is, I think I like Calvin," I say softly, feeling a little shocked that the words came out of my mouth.

"Oh."

I pull my towel more tightly around my body. "I wanted to tell you, because I just figured you should know."

"Thanks," he says. He looks down.

I wait for him to bring up the Micayla thing again, but he doesn't. I wait for him to bring up pretty much anything else, but he doesn't.

"Remember that kiss thing?" I ask him. "We talked about it during the year, about being each other's first kiss?"

He shrugs a little. As if maybe he remembers. Or maybe he doesn't.

"I just don't think it's the right time," I explain. "Like, I know we planned it. But is it okay if we don't do it?"

"Yeah, sure. Whatever. No big deal." He throws a piece of banana into the air and catches it in his mouth. "Your backstroke is a lot better than it was a few weeks ago."

"Thanks."

"Listen, I gotta run," he says. He seems uncomfortable and starts down the path to the sidewalk.

"Wait, Bennett," I call.

He turns around.

"We're still friends, right?" I ask.

He nods and then keeps walking.

"No matter what?" I ask, pleading.

He gives me a thumbs-up, high in the air, with his back to me.

I wish I could see his face.

After yet another rainy day with the dogs, I asked Claire if she wanted to get ice cream, just the two of us. I knew we needed to talk.

She seemed to be in a good mood, too.

But then things took a turn. I've realized that happens lately. You think that everything is fine, or manageable at least. And then, out of the blue, something changes.

We're walking along Main Street, and I turn to take her down one of Seagate's secret-alley streets that leads to a path to the beach. We need a quiet place to talk.

"It's just so unfair," she says. "Last summer I didn't want to be here at all, but this summer I was so pumped. And then my parents completely ruined everything."

"Even though I can't totally understand what you're going through, I still really want to help. I hope you know that," I say.

She nods. "I wish I could be anyone else but myself."

"Come on, Claire," I say. "You don't mean that. You're awesome. You say what's on your mind. You're a great friend. You're funny. You're smart."

"Thanks." She shrugs. "You don't realize how much your family defines you until your family breaks apart. I didn't appreciate it enough when my parents were together. But then again, a lot of the time it was bad. They would argue, and my dad would storm out. So why do I miss that? I don't get it."

I think about it for a second, trying to make sense of what she's saying, trying as hard as I can to find an answer. "I guess you miss it because even though it was bad, it was what you were used to," I say. "It's what was normal."

"I guess." She gets quiet, as if she's too tired to keep talking.

"What does Calvin say about it all?" I ask. "I can't tell how he's feeling about what's going on."

"He doesn't seem that bothered by the whole thing. He just accepts everything as it is and moves on," she says. "That's the way he is. Why do you care about him, anyway?"

My throat clenches. "He's my friend, too."

"You like him, Remy. I know you do. And he likes you." She stops walking and stares at me. "I wish you weren't pretending otherwise."

"What? Come on, Claire." Why do I feel that everything I do is wrong, when all I want to do is help?

"You keep secrets, Remy. And that's not fair to your

friends. And how do you think Bennett will feel about this?"

I stay quiet, because I can't think of anything to say. I should tell her that I told Bennett, but, truthfully, I just want this conversation to end. This feels like a game of dodge-ball, but Claire's the only one with the ball, and I'm standing against a wall with nowhere to go.

"Whatever, Remy. I don't get you," she says, and she walks away.

I've hurt Bennett, I've hurt Micayla, and now I've hurt Claire, too.

Halfway home, I feel a tap on my shoulder. I turn around, and it's someone who might be able to help me, though I hadn't thought of him until now. Actually, I've barely seen him all summer. Maybe that's why everything feels so mixed up.

I start to cry as soon as I see him.

"What's wrong?" Mr. Brookfield asks.

I mutter a quiet "Nothing."

"Come on. We both know it's not nothing."

We walk for a few minutes and then sit down on a bench outside SGI Sweets.

"Just tell me. I don't have all day." He laughs and nudges me with his shoulder.

"It's Claire," I tell him. "I'm really worried about her."

The truth is, it's not only Claire who's on my mind, but that's a good place to start.

"I am, too," he says. "I'm worried about the whole family. My daughter is really struggling. She's so sad. Divorce isn't good for anyone, not even people's pets. Clementine the hamster seems distressed, and I'm not sure where Baxter the bird is going to live."

I smile, but I don't think he's trying to be funny.

"Well, how can we help?" I ask him. "I try to be supportive, but everything I say to Claire is wrong, and I feel like she's always yelling at me."

"I know." He crinkles his eyes against the sun and looks at me. "Claire yells because she needs to get out her frustrations. She's not really yelling at you; she's yelling at the world."

"It's not fun," I say. "I can take it, but not all the time."

"She shouldn't yell at you. She shouldn't yell at anyone. But sometimes I think her yelling is a better way of handling it. Calvin keeps it all inside. He's hurting, too, but he doesn't talk about it," Mr. Brookfield tells me.

"So you're saying that yelling is a good idea?" I ask.

"No." He pulls up his socks. "But it's never a good idea to keep everything inside, either. Somewhere in the middle would be better."

"I guess we can try to help each of them find a better way to express their feelings."

"We can," he says. "But it takes time. It'll be a while before they feel comfortable with the new way of things."

"So what can they do? I mean, besides getting their feelings out?" I don't know why I expect Mr. Brookfield to have the answer. But all I want right now *is* an answer. A solution. Some kind of instructions to follow.

"Keep putting one foot in front of the other," he tells me.

"Really?" I ask.

"Yes. That's the secret to life, really. One foot in front of the other. Eventually you will get somewhere."

When I get home, Bennett is sitting on my front porch with my dad, working on a crossword puzzle.

"I won't interrupt you guys," I say, about to go inside.

My dad looks up. "No problem. We just finished."

Bennett and I look at each other and then down at our feet.

My dad says, "Well, I think Mom needs my help in the kitchen. She's working on some kind of fancy frittata."

I smile. My mom hates it when my dad helps in the kitchen, and he knows that I know that, but it was a good excuse anyway. I guess he could sense the tension in the air.

"I realized I wasn't done with the conversation we started the other day," Bennett tells me.

"Okay."

"Let's just get everything out in the open," Bennett says.

"Um . . ." My voice trails off, and I can't make eye contact with him. This is becoming the hardest day of my life, and I didn't see it coming. My whole philosophy on going with the flow and appreciating life's surprises is flying out to sea.

"I guess I thought things were going to be different between us this summer," he continues. "Like, I came with all these plans, that just the two of us would hang out, but then you didn't want any part of that."

"That's not true," I say quietly.

"It is." He scratches his cheek, classic Bennett nervousness. He doesn't get nervous often, but when he does, it's really obvious. "I had to force you into the swimming lessons. And every time I ask if you want to pick up the dogs together, you make some excuse. And you're so busy talking to Calvin all the time that you ignore me."

"I came to Seagate this summer thinking the same things you did. I spent all year thinking about you."

"You did?" he asks hopefully.

"Yes. But then I realized I need you to be my friend," I say. "That's really what's most important to me."

"Well, what changed?"

I try to think of how to explain it. "I don't know what changed. I guess I just like us being us, the way we've always been. It's what feels natural to me. I don't want that to change. Not even a tiny bit. Everything seems to be changing around us . . . I guess I'd like for our friendship to stay the same. It's one of my favorite things about my summers at Seagate."

Bennett nods slowly, as if understanding.

But there's something else I need to say. "If you like me so much, then why did you tell Calvin to go for it when he told you he liked me?"

He shakes his head, frustrated. "Okay, first of all, I don't know how you know that. And second of all, what was I going to say? He's my friend, too."

"I know," I say.

"Besides, I thought you liked *me*, so it didn't matter if Calvin liked you," Bennett says.

"I do like you, Bennett. I like you as a friend. You'll always be my friend. Okay?"

"Okay." He gets up and turns his Mets cap brim from front to back. "Talk to you later, Remy."

I watch him walk down the steps of my front porch, the way I've watched him so many times before. And I know he's not leaving for good, but for some reason it feels that way.

I stay out on the front porch until Dad comes and tells me that it's dinnertime and I should get excited because this frittata is going to be the best thing I've ever eaten.

Amazing frittata or not, I don't have the heart to tell him that I'm not hungry.

The next day, it feels as if everyone is ignoring me at Dog Beach.

Everyone but the dogs. They're still happy to see me, jumping up to give me kisses, wagging their tails, running in circles around me.

And Lester stays by my side the whole day. We had this long chat after the Larry Park performance, and he's been running away less. I guess his owner was right—he really does understand English. Sometimes owners say things about their dogs, and we listen and smile, but we don't believe them. But in this case, Lester's dog-dad was right.

Lester needed someone to understand him, and I guess I'm that person. I'm not sure the cocker spaniel understands me as well as my last dog, Danish, did, or as well as Marilyn Monroe does, but he sure comes close.

It also seems as if Calvin knows that something's up but doesn't know what, exactly, or what to do. I'm not sure how he can seem so in tune and smart sometimes and other times seem completely clueless or distant.

"Hey," he says, sitting at the edge of my lounge chair. Lester is on one side of me, and Marilyn Monroe is on the other, and I'm staring at the ocean, letting my mind wander.

"Hey," I reply.

"So, listen, I need to talk to you. I think Micayla told you that I liked you. And, no matter how you feel, I just don't want anything to get weird," he says, picking at the skin near his thumbnail.

I sit up. "You haven't made anything weird."

He nods halfheartedly. "Yeah, but we're a group of friends, and you and Bennett have your own thing going on, and I don't want to get in the middle of that."

"You're not in the middle. And Bennett and I don't have anything going on."

"You don't?"

"No. But you're a person, too, Calvin. You can have your own feelings and opinions. Why don't you tell me how *you* feel?"

"I like you," he says.

"And I like you, Calvin," I say. This is a rare moment when I'm not second-guessing what I'm saying. "I like talking to you. And I like listening to you talk. I like hanging out with you."

"Okay." He smiles. "Me too."

I laugh. "It's good you like spending time with yourself."

"You know what I mean," he scoffs. "I like all of those things about *you*."

I say, "Okay, good."

Then Calvin kneels down and says, "Lester, want to come play Frisbee?" Lester's on a leash attached to my lounge chair. He looks at Calvin and then turns away. "C'mon. Join the fun." He frees Lester's leash.

Finally the cocker spaniel agrees and follows Calvin over to the other dogs.

I get all the midmorning treats ready and play back that conversation in my head. So, Calvin and I like each other.

Now what?

Bennett is across the beach, giving Potato Salad a belly rub. For a few seconds, our eyes meet. He shrugs. I shrug.

It seems that we're having a conversation with our eyes, but I'm not entirely sure what we're talking about.

All I want to know is that everything is okay between us, that no matter what happens, everything will work out. That we'll always be Bennett and Remy. A friendship that started at the very beginning and went on forever.

I wonder if that's too much to ask. Maybe life is a series of events, and you can't know if things are always going to be okay. It's just one more thing I can't plan for.

I'm walking Atticus and Rascal home when Claire comes up behind me. "Here's the thing." She sniffles. Sometimes she jumps right in and starts conversations in the middle. I guess that's what happens when you know someone will listen.

I'm not entirely sure what I'm expecting her to say, and my stomach twists with anticipation.

"I feel like the whole world around me is just going on as if nothing has happened."

I nod, so she'll know I understand what she's saying.

"It doesn't seem fair." Tears trickle down her cheeks; she rubs them away with her palms. "How can the world just go on like normal when my parents aren't together anymore?"

I know she's not really asking me for the answer. But it feels as if I should know it. I wish I did.

"It seems like everything should stop," I say. "Like no one should have the chance to be happy ever again." I look at her. "Right?"

She sobs. "Right."

"Like everyone in the entire world should know how bad you're feeling. And it doesn't make sense that everything around you seems exactly the way it was before all this happened."

She sobs and sobs and sobs. "I'm so sad, Remy! I don't want it to be this way."

I put my arm around her and we walk that way for a while. I think about what Mr. Brookfield said: *One foot in front of the other. Eventually you will get somewhere.* And even though I'm not saying anything, I feel as if I'm helping a little. I listen to the soft patter of our flip-flops on the pavement, moving forward, and I know that together we will get somewhere.

29

The Seagate Centennial Summer celebration is three days away, and the whole island is excited. At least that's how it feels to me.

All the Adirondack chairs have been taken off the lawn by the ferry terminal to make room for the carnival rides and booths. The temporary stage has been set up way back on the lawn. It's perfect, really. That way everyone who's watching the performances also has a view of the ocean.

Mrs. Pursuit asks all the volunteers to meet her there so she can discuss how everything will work.

On my walk over, I think about what I'm going to say to Calvin. Maybe I should tell him that I don't know what to do now that we like each other. Or maybe I should ask him if he wants to go to Sundae Best this afternoon. Or is that too much like a date? Whatever. There's never a wrong time for ice cream.

When I get to the lawn and sit down on the grass with the rest of the volunteers, I turn around every few minutes to see if Calvin's coming up the path. But there's no sight of him. Did he forget? I check my phone. Nothing. Maybe he thinks I can handle getting all the information and that I'll tell him about it later.

Finally Mrs. Pursuit starts the meeting. She hands out a little map of where everything's going to be on the lawn and asks if we have any last-minute changes.

"Hi." Bennett plops down on the grass next to me. He's out of breath.

"Oh, hi," I say.

He starts scratching and scratching a mosquito bite on his ankle. "Calvin's stuck at home. Something about his mom having a rough morning. She had another fight over the phone with his dad." He squints. "So he asked if I could come and get the information for him."

"Oh." A tiny part of me sinks like one of those weighted rings we throw to the bottom of the pool, only to have to swim way down to get it. I wonder why Calvin didn't ask *me* to get the information.

"It's okay, Remy." Bennett laughs. "I can handle it."

"I know you can," I say a bit defensively.

"So the rides will be brought in tomorrow, the booths will be put in place after that, and you're welcome to set up your booth any way you'd like," Mrs. Pursuit says. "Be creative! I know you will be. Seagaters always are." She looks down at her papers and then back up at the crowd. "I think that's about it. Go enjoy the sunshine. Oh, one other thing. Is Remy Boltuck here?"

I stand up and wave. "I'm here." My nervous laugh squeaks out.

"Great. Anything we need to know about the performances?"

I shake my head. "I don't think so. We're all set."

"Wonderful. Thank you."

After that, everyone mills about, chatting and discussing plans for their booths.

"So, you and Calvin are really running a wedding booth?" Bennett asks me, standing up and brushing the grass off the butt of his shorts.

I nod and stay sitting for a few more seconds.

"Kind of weird, no?" he asks, looking down at me.

"Well, yeah," I admit, and I finally stand up. "He suggested it. I guess it was on his mind because of the situation with his parents. And he saw one at a carnival once and thought it was kind of funny."

"Oh. Got it."

"I'm going to pick up Marilyn Monroe at my house, then Lester and Oreo," I tell him. "See you at Dog Beach?"

"Yup."

Even though we've kind of said good-bye, we keep walking together, which feels a little awkward.

"Why do you look so worried?" Bennett asks.

"I do?" Now I'm all self-conscious. As if he told me that the back of my dress was stuck in my underwear.

"Yes."

"I feel like you're mad at me," I say. "And I really hate that feeling."

He groans. "I'm not mad at you. Come on."

"See? Now you're mad at me because I *think* you're mad at me."

He shakes his head, half frustrated, half amused. "Seriously. Stop."

I know I'm annoying him. But sometimes even when you know you're annoying someone, you can't stop doing it.

"I just didn't want to lose what we had." I keep talking, even though I know I should stay quiet. "I was trying so hard to keep everything the same that I actually made it different."

"You can't stop things from changing, Remy."

"So then why do you still seem annoyed at me?"

"Because I like you. As more than a friend." Even though he's talking about something nice, the words come out sounding snarly. "Because I'm annoyed that you wouldn't give us a chance, just because you were worried about losing our friendship."

I don't respond. He has a point, but I'm not sure I agree with him.

"My mom was always so scared of losing this ring she loved that she never wore it. She kept it at home in her dresser drawer," he tells me. "It was the stupidest thing ever. What's the point of even having the ring if it stays in a drawer?"

I think I understand what he's saying. "That's pretty dumb," I mumble. "And your mom's a smart lady."

"Sometimes you have to take a chance," he says.

"You're right," I say.

"I'm mad that you wouldn't give *us* a chance. And I still like you. *Like* you, like you, I mean. But I'll always be your friend. No matter what."

After a few moments of silence, we start to walk in different directions to pick up all the dogs. I keep thinking about what Bennett said. I didn't want to give him a chance, because what if it all fell apart and we lost what we had? But I know in my heart that there's another reason, too. I started to like Calvin. And you can't always help who you like. It just sort of happens to you. The same way you can't help who your parents are, and if they stay married or if they get divorced.

There's so much that we don't have any control over.

And that just seems so hard.

I look up at the sky, half expecting to see storm clouds looming in the distance.

On the way to Dog Beach, I stop at Mornings
to pick up some croissants. We all need some cheering up, especially Calvin and Claire.

I place the croissants on one of the lounge chairs and let all the dogs off their leashes. Well, except for Lester, who's acting feisty today.

"Who's on Lester duty?" Micayla asks.

"I guess me." I smile. "We seem to get each other."

"That makes sense," Micayla replies. "You both kind of like running away."

I think about her words, but I'm not totally convinced she's right. "I know I avoid change, but I haven't been running away as much lately. I've actually been opening up about my feelings. Especially with Calvin. Don't you think so?"

"Kind of." She pulls up the lounge next to me and lies

down. We watch Calvin and Bennett in the ocean with the dogs for a while. Every few seconds we see Oreo's black and white body pop up from the water.

His swimming has really improved.

"What do you mean, *kind of*?" I ask.

She waits a few seconds to talk. "Well, I still feel like you're avoiding how you really feel about Bennett."

"Stop already, Mic." Frustration seeps out, even though I don't want it to. "My feelings changed. I can't help it."

"So then it's fine for me to like him?"

It should be fine, but it's not. And I have no idea what to do about that.

"Why aren't you answering me?" she asks.

"Because I don't know what to say," I admit. "I'm sorry. It doesn't seem fine to me. But I don't know why."

She shakes her head and gets up to go help Calvin and Bennett with the dogs. Tabby and Potato Salad are growling at each other.

"Hey," Claire says, holding Ritzy in her arms. "Someone forgot to pick her up today."

"Oops." I look over the schedule. "It was me."

"I know," Claire scoffs. "You're too busy thinking about my brother and not focusing on your responsibilities."

Her words sting.

"Sorry." I refill the water bowls, mostly so I don't have to look at Claire. I know I messed up, but she doesn't have to be so mean about it.

She puts Ritzy down and gives me an angry look. "Honestly, Remy, I love you, but it's hard to be around you right now."

"What? Why?"

"You like my brother and he likes you." She scowls. "It's not okay. It makes me uncomfortable."

"I didn't plan it like this," I admit. "Honestly."

"So what? That doesn't change it. How come everything has to change around me, and I have to just go along with it?"

"I'm sorry," I say, even though I'm not sure I am.

"Uh-huh." She rolls her eyes. "Whatever." She walks off and joins the others, too.

How can Micayla and Claire both be so angry with me on the same morning?

Later that day, after all the dogs are home, I turn around with Marilyn Monroe and head to Daisy's for a treat, just the two of us. It's drizzling, but I don't even bother to take an umbrella. I've gotten so used to the rain this summer that I barely feel it anymore.

"We need some quality time," I tell Mari. "Right?"

She yips.

I get her one of Daisy's specialties, the doggie fruit salad: crunchy pieces of kibble in the shape of different fruits. She loves it. And I get a strawberry smoothie. We stay there for a while, hanging out, just the two of us.

"Everyone hates me," I whine to her.

She whimpers and goes back to her doggie fruit salad.

"I guess I messed up," I say. "It's weird to like your friend's brother."

Mari finishes her fruit salad and hops up into my lap while we wait for the check.

"It's easier to be a dog," I tell her. "Humans make things all complicated."

She nuzzles my neck and gives me a million doggie-lick kisses. Maybe she's saying that she thinks being a human is pretty great. Or maybe she's saying that dog life really is better. Or maybe she's simply the only one who understands me.

Calvin and I make a plan to meet at the grassy lawn to help set up. He's the only one in the group who's not mad at me at the moment, and I'm excited to spend some one-on-one time with him.

It's a little weird that we had that whole "we like each other" talk and then haven't hung out since. Maybe he doesn't know what to do about it, either. It's not as if there's any rule book to follow or anything. There's no way to prepare for these feelings.

On my walk over, the whole island feels off. There aren't many people around. I chalk that up to the fact that they're probably already busy setting up booths, or they're home preparing for the big day. Or maybe it's the weather.

It's gloomy out, gray and cloudy, the way it's been so many days this summer. There's once again been talk of a storm moving up from the south, and it's windy, the kind of wind that makes you want to pull the hood of your sweatshirt over your face.

I get that nervous feeling in my stomach, uneasy because my friends are mad and I'm not quite sure how to fix things. I push it away. This is Seagate Centennial Summer day! One hundred years of Seagate magic. I just know it's going to bring out the best in everyone. I need to focus on that.

I've been avoiding the great lawn the past few days because I didn't want to spoil the excitement of this moment. I didn't want to see the carnival rides or booths half set up. I wanted to see them all perfect and ready to go. I wanted to witness the complete picture.

But what I see is not what I anticipated. What I see looks like complete chaos.

"Remy!" Mrs. Pursuit says, clearly as startled as I am. She's in the process of quickly stuffing some materials into cardboard boxes and stacking them in one of the famous Seagate red wagons. "You shouldn't be here now."

"What? Why? What's going on?" I look all around. The carnival rides are dismantled and pushed together in a corner of the lawn. Only a few booths are standing. The stage is gone. "What's happening?"

"You haven't heard?" she asks me.

This feels like a bad dream. But this time I know I'm awake.

"We're evacuating Seagate." She continues stacking the boxes. "Today."

I look around. "We are? Why?"

She doesn't look at me. She keeps packing and stacking, out of breath, as if she's in some kind of imaginary competition. "The hurricane down south changed course. It's coming directly here. Mandatory evacuation for everyone."

"But the carnival! The Centennial," I say. "I don't get it."

"I know, Remy." She shakes her head and looks up at me finally. "But you need to get home. Go find your parents."

Come to think of it, it was a little weird that my parents weren't home this morning. I figured they were on one of their beach walks. But it's pretty odd that they didn't wake me up to tell me the bad news.

I text my friends as I run back home, but no one responds. Maybe they're all too busy packing. Maybe they left last night and didn't tell me? They're all mad at me, but they would still want to say good-bye, wouldn't they?

I run faster than I've ever run before. I don't understand what's happening right now. Everything changed so quickly. Everything we had planned is now ruined.

I get home, and my parents are out on the front porch, waiting for me.

"What part of stay here and start packing didn't you understand?" my dad asks me. He's angry. He doesn't get angry very often, so when he does, you definitely know it.

"What? I don't know what you're talking about."

He shows me the note. "We left this for you on the kitchen table."

"I didn't see it," I tell them. "I had no idea what's going on."

I'm so consumed with my own thoughts that I can't focus on anything my dad is telling me. Something about their going to get plywood planks to put over the windows. Sandbags. That's where they were this morning. They thought I understood when they half woke me from a sound sleep, but I'd promptly drifted back off and had no idea.

He explains that there are extra ferries leaving the island.

But I don't want extra ferries. I don't want to leave.

I can't leave Seagate knowing that Micayla and Claire are mad at me and that Bennett's annoyed with me, too. And when everything's still so confusing with Calvin.

And no Seagate Centennial Summer celebration. No carnival. What about the booths? The performers?

My dad continues. "A massive hurricane is brewing, coming up the coast. It looks like it will hit us directly in the next few days."

"No. Come on. They always say stuff like that," I explain. "Seriously. Nothing ever *really* happens. We don't need to go."

"It's real, Rem," my mom says. "It's not safe to stay. Safety comes first."

"What about the safety of Seagate? The houses? The stadium? Sundae Best?" I ask. "What's going to happen to them?"

My dad goes on and on about precautions—plywood planks and technical stuff that's too confusing to pay attention to.

"What about the year-rounders?" I ask them. "Where will they go?"

"There are shelters off-island," my mom tells me. "They have places to go. All the emergency precautions are in place."

"I can't believe summer is ending in early August."

My dad sighs. "Rem. We need to stay safe. That's all that's important."

"But we planned the whole carnival," I insist. "It was today. The Centennial Summer. All the performers. The booths. The rides."

"I'm sorry," my mom says. "No one is happy about this."

"This isn't fair! What about all our plans? All our hard work? Just for everything to fall apart?"

They sit quietly and look at each other, exasperated expressions on their faces.

"It's not fair that Calvin and Claire's parents have to get divorced! It's not fair that my friendship with Bennett might change. It's not fair that the dogs have had to spend most of the summer indoors!" I yell. "And now, out of nowhere, we're leaving today? I don't get it."

"None of us expected this, Remy," my mom says. "We thought it would blow over. And it sounds like you've had more than a storm to worry about this summer."

I nod sadly, and she comes to put an arm around me. Which helps a little.

"So now what?" I ask.

"Pack your stuff, Rem," my dad says. "I want to be on the two o'clock ferry."

"I gotta go find my friends," I say. "I need to say good-bye."

"Remy, please," my mom begs. "I don't want you running around outside. It's pouring."

"I'll be fine," I tell them on the way out.

"No, Remy!" My dad raises his voice. "You're staying home. Enough is enough."

I run up to my room and fall onto my bed. Within minutes, my pillowcase is drenched in tears. Seagate could be ruined forever, and there's not a single thing any of us can do about it.

We pack up as much as we can and head to the ferry. The intense rain and wind have already caused power outages and downed wires.

It looks as if the entire island is crying. The store signs look sad. The houses look gloomy. Even the Adirondack chairs look as if they're in mourning.

I want to apologize to everything on Seagate—all the buildings, the boardwalk, and the residents, furry and otherwise. *I'm so sorry we couldn't protect you. I'm so sorry we're leaving you here all alone.*

I go to check my phone to see if I've heard from anyone, and that's when I realize my phone battery has run down. There's no way to charge it now.

I pray that my friends will be taking the same ferry as we are, but I have no way to be sure. I don't even know where

Micayla and her family will go. And I don't know if Calvin and Claire are going back home or to their dad's new place in Manhattan.

Calvin and I didn't get to run our booth. We didn't even get to spend any time together.

I search for my friends through the raindrops. But I don't see them. I don't see anyone I know. Not even Mrs. Pursuit. Or Josh and the Improvimaniacs.

Did they take an earlier ferry?

I lug my wheelie suitcase up the ferry steps and sit down in the first seat I see. I cover my eyes with the hood of my sweatshirt. I can't watch this. I can't say good-bye. I can't believe I'm leaving Seagate when all my friends are mad at me and I have no idea when I'll see them again.

"Remy!" someone yells. I blink and pull back my hood.

"Remy! We can't find Lester!"

His owner-mom is shaking, crying. "Do you have any idea where he might be? We were packing up the house, and we had everything and everyone, and then he was gone!"

I need to think fast.

"Please, Remy. Do you have any idea?"

I think back to our many days spent at rainy-day head-quarters. At Dog Beach. Where did Lester most like to go? He liked to steal breakfast sandwiches and take them to the bookstore, but no one is eating any breakfast now for him to steal. He liked that sunny corner in the lobby of the old Seagate Hotel, but he wouldn't be able to get in. Wait! What if Lester went to the hotel, and he's sitting outside, getting soaked in the rain?

"I think I know!" I yell. "Follow me!"

"Remy, what are you thinking?" my mom asks. "Sit down this minute."

"We can't leave without Lester," I explain.

"Sit down right now, young lady," my dad says.

They yell, but I don't listen.

Sometimes in life you don't have a choice. You have to do what you have to do. I jump off my seat and run to the ferry driver. "I need ten minutes," I say. "It's a missing-dog emergency."

He raises an eyebrow but then shows a hint of a smile. "Ten minutes," he says. "I had a dog once. I understand. But I can't give you a minute more."

"Thank you!" I cry.

"Ten minutes, Remy," my mom says.

I nod. "We'll make it." Lester's owner-mom and I sprint across the island. The rain pelts our faces. Our clothes are as soaked as if we'd just jumped into the ocean. We run past Breakfast by the Boardwalk, past Mornings, past Frederick's Fish, past the stadium.

Everything is boarded up. Everything is closed. I don't know how it's possible for a place that always looks so happy to look so completely sad.

Please be there, Lester. Please be where I think you are.

I peek into a window of the old Seagate Hotel, just in case he's somehow gotten inside. Nope.

I look around the building. No sign of him. Where could he be? I think of poor Lester tugging on his leash, trying to break free. And I wonder what makes him so sad all the time, so restless.

I remember how happy he was singing along with Larry Park, as if he were born to perform classical music, barking along so sweetly. And then it hits me. The music. The beautiful classical music.

"There's one more place we need to check," I tell her.

His owner-mom looks at me hopefully.

When we get there, the store is boarded up. The one-dollar-books cart is gone.

I go to look under the bench, but the bench is gone.

Of course Mr. Aprone wouldn't leave a wooden bench outside during a hurricane.

But right there, huddled in a ball, exactly where the bench used to be, is Lester.

"Lester!" his owner-mom says. "Lester, Lester, Lester." She scoops him up and covers him with hugs and kisses. She says his name over and over again.

"How did you know he'd be here?"

"Lester loves the classical music Mr. Aprone plays in Novel Ideas. *That's* the reason he runs away all the time—he wants to listen to the music. Did you know that he loves to sing, too?"

She smiles and hugs the cocker spaniel, so relieved that he's safe. "Lester does love to sing. He always used to bark along when my daughter played piano . . . but now the piano is gone. I guess there hasn't been much reason for him to sing lately. From now on, there's going to be a lot more music in the house."

"That sounds like a great idea." I reach down and hug Lester, too. "Come on—we gotta go," I tell her.

Together, we sprint back to the ferry. Our ten minutes are almost up.

"Remy, are you okay?" my mom asks.

"Remy found him," Lester's owner-mom says. "She found Lester!"

"He wasn't lost," I say. "He knew we'd come and get him. He knew we'd know where to find him."

"I'm proud of you for finding the dog, Remy," my dad says, "but running off at a time like this was *not* the smart thing to do. We were so worried."

It sounds as if he's talking about Lester, but he's talking about me.

"I can't believe no one's on our ferry," I tell my mom when my parents take a break from lecturing me. "And my phone battery died. I never said good-bye to anyone."

"It's okay, Rem." She rubs my back. "You'll call them when we get back to the city. Everyone was rushing around, and there wasn't time for phone calls."

"What about Micayla?" I ask. "Where are the Walcotts going? Shouldn't we have offered to let them come with us? What if—"

She interrupts me. "The Walcotts are okay. They're going with the Newhouses. They'll ride out the storm in Boston."

I'm jolted by the thought of Mic staying with Bennett's family. "Really?"

She nods. I know she doesn't understand why this is a big deal. And I don't want to be the one to explain it to her. All that really matters is that Micayla and her family are safe, but Micayla should be with me.

I look out the ferry window as Seagate Island gets farther and farther away. I just hope it's not forever. Not knowing is, once again, the worst part.

Marilyn Monroe sits on my lap, and I hug her as tightly as I possibly can.

"Maybe they're on this ferry," I say to my mom a few minutes later. "Just because we didn't see them getting on doesn't mean they're not here."

She nods again. "Maybe."

Even my mom seems nervous. She's quiet. In fact, the whole boat is quiet. People don't say much during very stressful times. Maybe it's because they're too busy worrying to talk.

"I'm gonna walk around and look for them," I say. I put Marilyn Monroe on my mom's lap. "Be back soon."

I look all over the boat. I keep thinking that I see Micayla and Bennett. I keep praying that I'll see them. Maybe if I imagine them on this boat, they'll be here.

But they're not.

In a way, I want to stay on this boat forever. I want to cling to it, because it's the only little bit of Seagate Island I have right now.

I know that eventually we'll get off the boat, and eventually the storm will end. But what I don't know is if my friends will ever talk to me again.

My mom puts her arm around me when I return to our seats. "I'm sorry all of this is happening," she says.

"It's not your fault," I say. "You can't control the weather."

"That's true. I can't control the weather," she agrees.

"How can we just go on like normal when everything feels so shaky? So uncertain?" I ask her.

"Because we don't have a choice. We can only do the best we can."

I look at her. She pets Marilyn Monroe and squeezes my arm.

"But how can we do the best we can when everything feels so scary?" I ask her.

"You're already doing the best you can, Rem." She raises her eyebrows. "You found Lester. I'm not pleased that you ran off in the rain, but even though the situation was scary, you trusted your instincts, and you made a choice. You did what you thought was right."

"Oh." I look down at my muddy flip-flops.

"That's how we get through the tough times," she tells me. "By doing what we know is right, and trusting that eventually things will be okay."

I rest my head on her shoulder. She smells like the ocean and sunscreen and the orange lotion she rubs on her hands every night before bed.

"Don't shower when we get home," I tell her.

"Why not?"

"I want you to smell like the beach for as long as you possibly can," I explain.

She smiles.

34

We get back to Manhattan, and it's raining there, too. The whole East Coast is being slammed, but some areas are safer than others.

Our apartment is hot and stuffy, as if someone pumped as much sticky air into it as they possibly could and then locked all the doors and sealed all the windows. Being back in the city in August just feels wrong.

Three days later, it feels like forever. I don't know how long we have to stay here; that in and of itself is unsettling.

But there's one tiny silver lining.

I charged my phone as soon as I got home. And when I did, a bunch of texts popped up.

From Bennett: *Be safe, Rem. See you soon. And in case you're wondering, of course we're still friends. Always.*

From Claire: *Even though you like my brother, I still*

love you. Agh. Why aren't you answering your phone? Call me pleaaaaasssseeeee.

From Micayla: *Where are you?!? Stop ignoring me. I've called you seventeen times. I love you. I hope you're safe!*

From Calvin: *I wanted to say good-bye. Hope we're back on SGI very soon. Maybe we can do the wedding booth next year.*

People do come together when disaster strikes. People let go of their grudges when there are more important things to worry about. I left Seagate fearing that everyone was mad at me, but what I learned is that they all really cared. So we've all been texting back and forth and updating one another every day.

Claire and Calvin are in Westchester, but if we get word that it's safe to go back to Seagate, they're going to beg to come back with their grandfather.

Claire's back to being the social planner for her friends at home. She says it keeps her mind off the sad stuff. And Calvin's trying to sell some of his old video games on eBay. He wants to raise money in case Seagate needs help getting back up and running.

Micayla and Bennett are doing okay in Boston, though she says it's awkward to see so much of him. She says he forgets she's around and eats breakfast in his underwear. So she pretty much keeps to herself there, reading on the porch.

It's funny how a person can be so different depending on where they are or who they're with.

But that's probably what makes life interesting. That we're not all the same all the time.

How boring would that be?

I'm lying on the couch, daydreaming about what it would be like if Calvin and Claire were in Manhattan right now, when my mom comes back from the grocery store.

"I have news," she says.

I sit up. Good news? Bad news? I can't tell.

"People have started going back to Seagate to assess the damage," she tells me.

"And?"

She puts the grocery bags on the table and sits down next to me. "It's bad, but not as bad as we feared."

"What do you mean?"

"The stadium needs a new roof. And the community pool has extensive damage," she says. "Some houses had first-floor flooding, but only the ones on the ferry side of the island."

"What are those people going to do?"

"They can stay upstairs while the first floors are being repaired," she says. "I haven't heard of any houses that are unlivable."

"This is great news!" I stand up. "Right?"

Sighing, she says, "Yes, it's good news. It could have been much, much worse."

"Nobody lost their homes. That's huge!"

She nods.

"And we can go back to Seagate?"

She hesitates. "Dad and I are still discussing that. There's lots of damage to be cleaned up. Fallen trees, buildings that might be in danger of collapsing. We're still not sure if it's the best thing to do."

"Mom," I plead, "we need to help clean it up. Isn't that obvious?"

She smiles. "We're going to think about it."

That's the best answer I'm going to get.

Micayla and her family go back to Seagate
first. The year-rounders and business owners need time to
get things up and running and secure their homes.

Micayla's house sustained minimal damage, mostly to
the front porch. It's sad, because I love Micayla's porch—it
wraps almost all the way around the house. But it could have
been so much worse. Again and again, I hear my mom saying
to people: *We were so lucky.*

She's right. But it all still feels sad to me. I discovered that
you can be grateful and sad at the same time. I guess I never
knew that was possible.

Even though Claire and Calvin and I have been texting,
I've been avoiding calling them. Not because I don't want to
talk, but because I'm nervous, I guess. I'm nervous because
Claire and I ended our last encounter on an angry note. And

I'm nervous that Calvin might have forgotten that he even liked me in the first place. But after the fourth day at home, I'm so bored and lonely that I can't resist calling their land-line, though I'm afraid Calvin could answer.

Thankfully, he doesn't.

"Hey, hey," Claire answers after the first ring.

"Hi, it's Remy, but I guess you know that. You have caller ID, I'm sure." Nervous laugh. "What's up?"

"Well," she begins, "Calvin's throwing a basketball off the roof of the house, and it's unbelievably annoying. My grand-father's snoring in the living room. My mom is on a business call. And I'm talking to you." She pauses. "That's what's up."

"Wow," I say. I tell her about Micayla's family going back to Seagate. "You guys are coming back, too, right?"

"I don't know," she says. "My grandfather and my mom want us to, but my dad is trying to get Calvin and me to come to Manhattan."

"Oh, right." I put my feet up on the coffee table. "How's that situation going?"

She's silent for so long, I think that the call has dropped. But no, she's still on the other end of the phone. She's crying.

"Claire, I'm sorry," I say. "I didn't mean to upset you. You sounded so—"

"It's weird without him here," she says. "It's weird being in the den and seeing the armchair he'd sit in; it's always empty now. And his seat at the kitchen table. The mugs he'd use for his coffee. It feels so lonely."

I don't know what to say to that.

I imagine how I'd feel if this happened to me. I'd feel terrible. I think about the newspaper; it would come every morning, but Dad wouldn't be there to rush to read it.

Claire changes the subject. "I should totally feel grossed out by you, because you have a crush on my brother." She hesitates. "And I do feel uneasy about it. But—and don't get all mushy about this—you're the best listener I know. I can't stay mad at you."

"Thanks," I say. I know how hard it is for Claire to be sweet sometimes.

"I need you, Remy," she says. "When we had to leave Seagate in such a hurry and you weren't responding to texts or answering your phone, I felt awful. I realized what a good friend you are. You listen to me babble and cry. And I know that I was no fun to be around this summer."

I stop her. "Claire, come on."

"I guess it's okay that you like my brother, even though it's weird, as long as you promise to still be my friend, too. Okay?"

"It's a deal," I say. "But you have to promise me that you'll come back to Seagate. I'm pretty sure we're going, even though my parents haven't officially told me yet. They'll need to check on the house anyway."

"I'll see what I can do," Claire says.

When my phone rings five minutes later, and I
see that it's Claire's number, I get excited. She must have
already found out they can go back to Seagate. That was
easy.

"Hey, so what ferry are you taking?" I ask.

"What?"

"Claire?"

It's not Claire. It's Calvin.

"Oh, hi."

My heart races. Like it's running a marathon.

I ask, "Is everything okay? Are you okay?"

"Yeah, I'm okay," he says hesitantly. "How are you?"

The only boy I've ever talked to on the phone is Bennett. And half the time we were playing Twenty Questions
or Would You Rather or Truth or Dare. But now I'm on the

phone and Calvin's on the other end. I don't know what to do.

"I'm good. Bored," I admit. "I really want to go back to Seagate. I miss it so much. I miss the dogs." I pause and realize I'm pretty much just saying anything that pops into my head. "I miss you, um, I miss you guys, too."

He says, "I want to go back. My grandpa will need help cleaning up his house and the yard and stuff. And there's nothing for us to do in Westchester."

"Tell me about it," I say. "I'm here now. For the city that never sleeps, it feels pretty sleepy."

"Let's FaceTime," he says with a little more pep in his voice. "I want to see your room."

"Really?" I ask. "It's nothing special. And it's kind of messy."

What I don't want to tell him is how disheveled my hair looks and that I'm still in my pajama shorts and T-shirt.

"Yeah. I don't care if it's messy. You can give me a tour of your apartment." He pauses. "It can be kind of like our first date. I mean, like, ya know, a phone date."

I didn't expect him to say something like that. But I think it's a good sign. Maybe he hasn't forgotten about liking me.

Soon he appears on my phone. He's there. Right there. Sitting on a leather couch, wearing a backward baseball cap.

I take him on a tour. It doesn't last very long. Kitchen. Main room. My room. My parents' room. Bathroom. Hallway. Done.

"That's it," I say. "I'm going to have a muffin. Care to join me?"

He laughs. "Sure. I'll pretend I'm sharing the muffin with you at Mornings. Not banana, right?"

"Nope. Blueberry."

"I hate banana muffins," he tells me.

"I'll never make you eat a banana muffin over the phone," I declare. "So no worries on that front."

I slice the muffin. "Here. Two pieces." I show him. When I look back at the phone, I realize he's switched places. He's in his room now. Maybe he needed more privacy.

I see a plaid comforter. An old desktop computer. Trophies on a shelf. A framed kindergarten diploma.

Looks like a pretty average room to me.

Calvin sits on his bed. His face is gloomy all of a sudden. Something has changed.

"Are you okay?" I ask, and then I regret it.

"You already asked me that."

We were having so much fun, and then something happened. I don't know what it is.

"Right. Sorry." I take teeny-tiny bites of my muffin.

Calvin takes me on a tour of his room.

And then more silence. I think we've run out of things to say already, and that makes me nervous.

I can't handle the silence anymore, so I start talking about the storm, what's left of Seagate, what the dogs might be doing. "Without seeing it for myself, I'm worried, you know?"

He nods but stays quiet.

"Do you know what I mean?" I ask. I could be talking to a door right now and it would be more satisfying.

"I do," he says quietly after what feels like a decade. There's another long silence. But then he starts talking. And he keeps going. "I know how you feel. You're trying to cling to something as tightly as you possibly can. But sometimes you can cling so tightly to something that it all just crumbles apart." He looks at me, tight-lipped. "Like that muffin. If you pick it up gently, it will stay together. If you pick it up and squeeze it, it's just a handful of crumbs."

I jump in. "Crumbs can still be delicious."

"Sure. If that's all you have," he answers. "But a whole muffin is way better. Isn't it?"

I nod.

"What I'm saying is that you're clinging to a Seagate summer too tightly," he tells me. "Your Seagate summer is a bunch of messy crumbs now."

"I see." I look down at my half-eaten muffin and realize I don't feel hungry anymore.

"I only know this because I've done the same thing," he says under his breath. He rubs his eyes, and I'm not sure if he's about to cry.

"What do you mean?"

"I tried to cling to my parents being together. I'd remind them of the fun things we did, how great everything was," he says. "I'd list things we had to look forward to as a family. I'd bring up memories and try to get them to reminisce."

"You did all that?" I ask. Marilyn Monroe jumps up onto my lap. She suddenly seems interested in this conversation, too. I guess she could hear Calvin's voice from the other room.

"Yes. I was always saying things like *We had so much fun that day*, like I needed to remind them of the good times. Because I didn't want to face that our family was broken."

I put down the piece of muffin. That may be the saddest thing I've ever heard.

"So believe me, I know about clinging to things," he says. "You think Claire's the only one who's upset and taking this hard? I am, too. In my own way."

"I know that," I say softly.

"But clinging to things doesn't make them stay. Because you're not in control. Sometimes things slip away from us, and we can't do anything about it. Just like the hurricane blew away parts of Seagate Island."

"I know that, too," I mumble.

I'm about to say something about Seagate and the storm when I realize we're not talking about that anymore. We're talking about Calvin and his family. He's opening up and telling me how he feels. I want him to keep sharing.

"There's nothing wrong with remembering the good stuff sometimes. It helps us get through the bad."

He nods. There's a glimmer in his eye, a glimmer of appreciation that he knows I understand him. He seems happy to get these thoughts off his chest.

We talk for thirty-seven minutes. That may be a record for FaceTime—a record for me, at least.

"I gotta go," Calvin tells me. "My mom needs help bringing in the groceries."

"I hope she didn't buy too much. Hopefully you'll be back on Seagate before you have time to eat all of it."

"If I have to eat all of it in a day, then, I will." He laughs. "Whatever it takes."

"Whatever it takes," I repeat.

When I come into the kitchen for breakfast the
next morning, banana-walnut pancakes are waiting for me at
the table. Also, a tall glass of fresh-squeezed grapefruit juice
and a bowl of strawberries.

This can't be good. I mean, it will be delicious, but I don't
think good news is coming. I think this is my parents' way of
buttering me up, only to let me down easy.

"What's this?" I ask them. They're sitting across from each
other, reading sections of the *New York Times* and drinking
coffee.

My mom looks up from the paper. "Just breakfast." She
smiles. "Sleep well?"

I nod. I don't believe her. It's definitely not *just breakfast.*
Just breakfast is an English muffin with jelly. Or a bowl of
Cheerios.

I'm only halfway done syruping my pancakes when my dad puts down the newspaper and starts talking. "Remy, we've been thinking it over. And we're not sure going back to Seagate right now is the best plan."

I knew it.

He continues. "There's a lot of damage around the house, and there was some flooding on the first floor. We're trying to schedule workers to come out." He pauses, as if it's painful for him to say all this. "Right now it's not the Seagate you know and love."

I put down my fork, and it clinks against the plate.

"Are you listening to yourself?" I ask. "This is Seagate Island. Our other home. Our community. We can't just abandon it because it's had a rough time, can we?"

My mom and dad look at each other.

"It's a tough call," my mom admits. "But the Seagate Community Council isn't encouraging people to come back right away."

"But Seagate needs our help! Not going back would be like ignoring Aunt Evelyn just because she can't walk like she used to," I explain. "Or giving up on a hard subject in school instead of trying to get better at it."

They consider that for a second but then continue explaining how there's going to be a lot of cleanup to do if we go back. It's not going to be carefree, the way it was before.

"I don't care," I say. "I'll help clean up as much as I can. I'll do whatever it takes."

"She has a point," my mom tells my dad.

He sighs. "I'll think about it."

My dad takes his plate and his coffee mug and puts them in the dishwasher. "I need to go to the office for a little while. Let's put this conversation on hold for now, okay?"

"Okay," I reluctantly reply.

I soak my pancake in the syrup that's pooling on the side of the plate and take the biggest bite I can. At least he didn't say no.

Either I'm really good at convincing people, or my parents can be worn down very easily. Hard to say for sure. But let's just put it this way: we're going back to Seagate!

We're on the ferry, and I keep thinking about how I felt the last time we were on our way to the island. I was filled with anticipation, and with a sense of not knowing what the summer would hold.

But it's different now. While we might not know exactly what's in store for us there, we know that Seagate will be different, and we'll have a lot of hard work to do to fix things up. But we aren't running away from that scary stuff; we're running right toward it.

The ferry is quiet, the mood of the passengers somber yet hopeful. People are chatting, discussing the storm, sharing stories, dispelling rumors. Someone thought the roof of Sundae Best had caved in. Not true, thank goodness!

We get off the boat, and I see Micayla right away.

I expect her to be her usual cheerful self, but something's different about her. She hardly smiles as she sees me and hugs me. "I'm so glad you're here," she says. "It's been so lonely."

And just like that, a gobstopper-sized lump forms in my throat.

My parents scoop up Marilyn Monroe and tell me to take my time with Micayla, that they'll meet me back at the house later. Maybe they want to assess the damage without me there. I'm not sure. But I'm grateful for some time alone with Micayla.

"It's like a ghost island now," she says. "I keep seeing you places, but you're not there. Not even Calvin and Claire are here. No Mason. No one."

"I'm here now," I remind her.

"I know. Thank God." She chews her pinkie nail for a second and then says, "I can't believe we got into a stupid fight over a boy. Over *Bennett*."

"Yeah, let's never do that again," I say.

We walk down Main Street, and we see the damage everywhere. Trees that used to stand tall and proud have fallen over, lying on their sides, as if they've given up.

Part of the stadium roof caved in and is now covered with blue tarp. The grills and picnic tables have been removed. The beach has eroded.

Only a few of the restaurants have opened back up. Mornings. Frederick's Fish. Pastrami on Rye. That's it.

Mr. Aprone hasn't come back yet, so Novel Ideas is still boarded up. Same with Sundae Best.

Micayla's right. It is a ghost island. Maybe I should have listened to my parents. Maybe we should have stayed home. Maybe dealing with the reality of this new Seagate will be too hard.

"So what's gonna happen now?" I ask her.

"Well, cleanup crews are here." She half shrugs. "That's what my dad said. But we can all pitch in with certain stuff, like cleaning up the beach."

My heart perks up. "That sounds good. Let's do that."

I'm happy that we have a plan.

"The school had some damage, too," Micayla tells me. "So I think it'll be a priority to fix that up so we'll be able to start classes on time in the fall."

I nod. We walk down to the beach and sit on the Adirondack chairs on the boardwalk. At least the Adirondack chairs are back. Seagate Island without Adirondack chairs is like a sundae without whipped cream, or a campfire without s'mores.

We look out at the ocean together, and for that instant, it feels as if my problems are so tiny that they don't even exist. I feel so lucky for everything I have. The sea is so vast that it makes me feel very small. Like I'm just a tiny little speck on the planet.

All I can do is try my best to make the world better.

Which reminds me of Bennett. I still need to make things right.

"I'm sorry about the Bennett thing," I say, continuing our conversation from before. I realize how selfish I've been. I do want Micayla and Bennett to be happy. "I don't know why I said that you couldn't like him. That was ridiculous."

"It's okay. I should have known it would be complicated for you, too."

"I just want you and Bennett to be my friends," I say. "That's it."

She leans back in the chair. "Well, you don't have to worry about that. We always will be."

"Good," I say.

"He's back, by the way," she says. "He asked about you, and I lied and said I didn't know when you were returning."

"Why?"

She answers matter-of-factly. "I wanted you to myself for a little while."

Something about that feels nice. But I feel my stomach knot up, knowing that Bennett is back. There seems to be so much space between us now. Too much.

"I don't like Bennett that way anymore anyway," she tells me. "After a few days with him in Boston, I realized that he's just a friend. There was too much nose-picking and slurping of cereal milk for me to be more interested than that!"

"But you've been watching him slurp his cereal milk for years."

"It's different on Seagate," she says.

She's right. On Seagate, even the most boring, run-of-the-mill things seem special. Even brushing your teeth on Seagate doesn't feel like a chore. Taking the garbage out offers a chance to see the ocean. Even watching a boy slurp cereal milk doesn't seem disgusting, because you're happy. And when you're happy, anything is possible.

"That's why we have to get the island back to the way it was before the storm." I sit up straight. "We need to do whatever we can."

"Remy," she groans. "I know that twinkle in your eye. You're plotting something."

"I am. But it's something we can totally do," I tell her. "Really."

On your first night back on Seagate Island after a hurricane, when everything feels empty, when your pool isn't safe for swimming, when you feel alone in your favorite place on earth, there's only one thing to do. Only one person to talk to: Bennett Newhouse.

I don't bother texting or calling, because I don't want to have to wait for a response. I don't want to give him a chance to ignore me.

Bennett's mom answers the door. She looks worn out, but she musters a smile. "Hi, Remy-roo!"

She's called me that since I was a baby, apparently, and I'd never admit it, but I love it. It means she knows me. Really knows me. There's something so special about a person who has known you since you were a baby and has more memories of you than anyone else does.

"Hey." I smile as I walk in. Their house always smells like cranberry scones. Morning, noon, and night. They're Mrs. Newhouse's favorite, and she's constantly baking on Seagate.

I wonder when they got back. I wonder how she already had time to bake. But maybe baking calms her down. "Is Bennett home?"

It seems quiet here. Too quiet for Bennett and Asher to be home, and it's too early for them to be asleep.

"I think he's out back," she says.

I walk through their den, where Bennett's dad is sleeping on the couch. I go out to their back porch. The furniture is gone, and the porch is covered with branches and sand and seaweed.

Well, this could be a good place to start the cleanup process.

I walk down the few steps to the beach. They don't have a pool, but they have a dock, and that makes up for it.

Bennett's on the dock, sitting forward on an Adirondack chair, bouncing a ball. It seems funny to only see one chair out here. The dock is usually covered with kayaks and rafts.

"Hey," I say quietly.

"Remy," he answers, sounding as if he's reading my name off an attendance sheet. "I didn't know you were back. I was just taking a cleanup break. I'm exhausted."

I sit down next to him on the dock. I pull my knees to my chest and look out. The ocean is so choppy that it almost frightens me. It's as if the sea is mad at someone and needs to take its aggression out on all of us. I always thought the ocean was calmer after a storm. Maybe not.

I stay quiet, wondering what to say. I'm not even sure why I came here exactly. Only that I needed to talk to Bennett. I need his calm reassurance. I need him to tell me that everything is going to be okay. That we're going to be able to clean up the island and bring it back to life.

"I'm sorry," I begin.

He looks at me. "For what?"

I shrug. "For being weird all summer. I think I took my time and my friends here for granted, which I never want to do. Putting off our swim lessons when I should have cherished every one. I thought I had more time than I did. And then, when we were gone, you felt so far away."

"That's kind of the way life is," he says, laughing a little. "We don't appreciate what we have when we have it."

"True." I bite the inside of my cheek. "Why is that?"

He shrugs. "Dunno." He throws a pebble into the water. "Sorry the whole carnival didn't happen. I know you were excited about that."

Truthfully, I'd kind of forgotten about it. It seems like such a small thing now.

There's so much to say and nothing at all to say at the same time. So I stay quiet. Being next to Bennett is comfort enough.

"So, what have you been doing since you've been back?" I ask.

"We just got here yesterday. I'm helping my mom clean up and, you know, just hanging. Thankful that I can even be here."

I nod in agreement.

"You planning to get the doggie day camp up and running?" he asks. "I haven't seen any of the dogs yet."

"I don't think so," I say. "Maybe next summer. But for now, I think we should focus on helping clean up the beach and doing whatever else we can."

"Sounds good."

"So you'll help?" I ask.

"Of course I'll help," he scoffs. "Like you even had to ask."

I smile. "So, where to start?"

"Right here." He laughs. "Get a broom!"

And just like that, things feel back to normal.

40

Claire texts me to let me know they're coming back to Seagate. She said she begged and begged and begged. And her grandpa had to go back anyway, and her mom didn't want him going alone. So it all worked out.

I text her back to say I'll meet them at the ferry.

I sit on the bench and wait for them, and it feels as if popcorn is popping in my stomach. In reality it's only been a few weeks since I've seen Calvin, but it feels like forever. We had that FaceTime chat, but we haven't talked since.

And seeing Claire is always a little nerve-racking, too. You never know what kind of mood she's going to be in.

I'm picking sand out of my flip-flop straps when I see them coming. Even though I'm nervous, I'm so excited that I start waving both arms.

"Remy!" Claire screams.

"Hey!" I yell back.

"It's so good to be back." Claire runs to me and gives me a hug. Then she stops and looks around. "Sheesh, it's depressing here. Everything is closed!"

"Well, not everything," I tell them. "A few things are open. Like Pastrami on Rye. How's your family?" I ask.

"I'm better," Claire says. "But Calvin hasn't been doing so great."

I look over at Calvin, who's pulling his suitcase off the ferry.

"Oh" is all I can manage to say. "We should wait for him to catch up."

"I've accepted the whole situation," Claire continues. "There's nothing I can do to change it. Now I want to try to enjoy what's left of the summer."

"We will," I say. "And we'll help others enjoy it, too."

"Wait, you said Pastrami on Rye is open?" she asks me, excitement in her voice. "I have to go get my mom and grandpa their favorite sandwiches! It will totally cheer them up!"

I nod. "Good idea!"

"Hi, Calvin," I say as soon as he gets to us. My stomach flips over.

All he says is "Hey."

"I'll see you guys later," Claire says. She runs off in the other direction, while her mom and Mr. Brookfield start walking to their house with the luggage.

"Claire went to get sandwiches at Pastrami on Rye for

your mom and grandpa. Which are their favorites?" I ask to break the tension.

"My mom's is turkey with coleslaw and Russian dressing. Like yours." He smiles. "My grandpa's is literally pastrami on rye. With mustard."

He laughs. I think he's perking up a little bit.

I laugh, too. "Good to know."

"Want to take a walk?" he asks.

Seagate might look a little different, but I'm still happy that we can take a walk through it. As we stroll through town, I see that the bench outside Novel Ideas is back.

Mr. Aprone must have returned to the island. Lester's going to be so happy when he sees this!

"Let's sit for a minute," I say.

Calvin and I are on the bench, side by side, and I wait for him to say more.

"It's okay to be sad," I say.

He half shrugs. "Yeah."

"You've gone through so much this summer. And you've kept it bottled up inside for a long time."

We stay quiet for a while. But it's nice to just be together, sitting on the same bench, thinking about things. Maybe that means we're comfortable with each other. Maybe that means we don't have to talk a lot for things to be okay.

"I still like you," he says, breaking the quiet. "Just so you know."

"Okay." I laugh. "That's good. I still like you, too."

"Well, that's something to not be sad about."

I'm glad to make Calvin happy, even if only for a moment.

"I should get home. Walk with me?"

I stand up, and he takes my hand.

Calvin and I walk together. Hand in hand. Block after block. Past empty stores and empty restaurants and fallen trees. I can feel my hand getting sweaty, but I don't want to let go.

We spend the next few days cleaning up debris as best we can. Mrs. Pursuit, Mr. Aprone, and the rest of the Seagate Community Council organize a meeting so they can go over what needs to be done and where volunteers should focus their efforts. Everyone seems really dedicated.

We try to help as much as we can, but people tell us that some areas aren't safe for kids, and we shouldn't be lifting heavy stuff. Hearing this again and again, it feels as if they don't really want our help.

Atticus and Rascal are the only dogs that are back. And Paul and Andi don't really need us to watch or entertain them. Josh and the Improvimaniacs are also back, and they're running theater classes for the few little kids who are here.

"We're just improvising," Josh says whenever he sees me, and then he laughs. He finds that comment really funny.

Improvising their way through the rest of the summer. Improvising their way through life. "That's what life is, Remy. Improvising."

He tries to be so deep, and it always makes me laugh. But then I get it. The Improvimaniacs *love* change. Their job is to react to it, to create a little magic from the unknown when it gets thrown their way. Suddenly I see their sketches and jokes in a whole new way.

I'm sitting outside Novel Ideas, feeling bad that we can't help more with the cleanup. Feeling sad for Calvin and Claire, sad for Seagate. And sitting here makes me miss Lester. He loved this spot. Underneath this bench was his favorite place on the island. It's weird without him here. I wonder if the Decsinis are coming back.

"Hey, Remy." Mrs. Pursuit sits down next to me. "You okay?"

"Yeah." I shrug. "I guess."

We sit there quietly, and I wonder how long she's going to stay. It feels funny, just Mrs. Pursuit and me on this bench, not talking, not even reading something we just purchased at Novel Ideas.

"I had an idea," she says finally. "Tell me what you think."

"Okay." I perk up. I'm always happy to listen to someone else's thoughts. It's good to have a break from my own.

"You were really helpful with all the Centennial Summer planning, even if it never happened. The island feels pretty empty now. I think we all need something to help us cheer up." She looks at me. "Should we try to get organized and see if we can pull off some smaller kind of celebration?"

"Really?" I ask.

"Yeah. What have we got to lose?"

"That's true."

"Will you and your friends help?" she asks.

"Absolutely!"

"Josh! J have an idea!" J shout when J get to the old Seagate Hotel, our former rainy-day headquarters. Thankfully, it didn't suffer any damage from the storm.

Standing in the doorway, Josh rubs his eyes with his palms and grumbles, "I just woke up."

"Oh. I'm sorry."

I give him a second to wake up, regretting that I didn't think to call first. Or at least text.

I tell him about Mrs. Pursuit's idea for a small Centennial celebration and explain that we need a place to have it. "The stadium's roof is damaged, and . . ."

"Uh-huh." I can tell his mind is wandering. I think he wants to go back to sleep.

"So, can we have it here?"

"Here?"

I nod.

"Hmm."

Please say yes. Please say yes. It's such a small thing, really. But right now it feels like a very big thing.

"Sure, why not?" he says with his eyes closed. "You might want to do it sooner rather than later, though. My mom and her sisters are coming back. They're in the process of selling the building. Some big hotel developer is buying it."

"What? Really?"

"Yup." He stares at me for a second. "I don't know why I'm telling you this. I think I'm still asleep." He closes his eyes and then opens them again. "Later, Remy."

As the days go by, more and more people come back to Seagate. Dogs, too. Tabby's back. So is Potato Salad. No sign of Ritzy, though. No Lester, either.

We offer to watch the dogs, and people seem appreciative. But it's not the same. One dog for an hour. Another later on. It's not camp anymore, really; it's more like babysitting. But it's better than nothing.

After an afternoon spent washing and brushing Tabby, I see Calvin down the block as I walk home.

"Hey, I was looking for you!" Calvin shouts.

"Yeah?" I ask.

Out of breath, he says, "I have amazing news! Sundae Best reopened." He pauses for a second to catch his breath. "I was thinking that, um, we could go together."

I let the good news wash over me. Sundae Best is open. Calvin wants to go together. Things really are looking up. "They're stocked and ready to go?"

"Yup. Come on." He grabs my hand.

I want to ask Calvin if this is, like, our first official date, since our FaceTime chat wasn't really a date. A date needs to be in person, two people face-to-face, I think.

But truthfully, I don't think it matters what we call it. It doesn't need a label, and neither do we.

"I'm so happy you're back," I tell Josie, Sundae Best's owner. "Seagate isn't Seagate without Sundae Best."

"Happy to be back," she says. "We don't have all the flavors yet, but we've got a pretty good selection. Give us a day or two and we'll be fully back in action."

"Did you guys have any damage to the store?" Calvin asks.

For some reason, this makes me really proud of him. I'm proud that he's so concerned about Josie and her ice cream shop. I'm proud that he cares about others enough to ask.

"Nope. We got very lucky," she says. "I was worried about the freezer being flooded. But I guess God loves ice cream." She laughs and points to the sign above the shop door that says ICE CREAM IS MY RELIGION. And we laugh together.

"Josie, may I have a Surprise Scoop?" I ask.

Calvin gasps. "Remy Boltuck, getting a Surprise Scoop?"

I like that he knows that about me, that I've never wanted to be surprised. That he knows, then, that this is a big deal. And that I *can* handle change.

"People change, Calvin." I lift my eyebrows, all self-assured. "People change."

I select my current favorite for the first scoop—chocolate milk and cookies—and Josie gives me banana marshmallow for the Surprise Scoop.

Delicious. Unexpected. A surprise.

Calvin picks mango sorbet and gets a Surprise Scoop of strawberry cheesecake.

So we sit, and we eat our ice cream. We have the whole shop to ourselves. Josie busies herself in the back, probably getting things organized, or maybe she wants to give us some privacy.

On the walk home, Calvin tells me that he's mastered something.

"What is it?" I ask.

"I've been practicing and practicing." He pauses, puts his hands on my shoulders, and looks right into my eyes.

Oh no. Is he talking about kissing? And he's been *practicing*? On other girls? No, that can't be. But I don't think I'm ready for this. "Wait, Calvin, I—"

"*Aaaaheeeeoowwww!*"

Despite his scream, I heave a sigh of relief. The biggest sigh of relief I've ever let out in my entire life.

He wasn't talking about kissing. He was talking about screaming. Mr. Brookfield's famous scream, to be exact.

"Wow," I say. "That was very impressive." I act nonchalant, as if I wasn't worried at all about having my first kiss in front of the statue of Melvin Jasper, the first person ever to come to Seagate Island.

"I knew you'd be proud," he says.

"I am. So proud."

We walk home, and Calvin tells me about how he's been practicing and that next summer he wants to help his grandpa with the Scream Contest. Last summer we had an amazing one, which not only was super fun but also let the entire island learn that Mr. Brookfield was in the movies. Or at least his scream was. But Mr. Brookfield is a real film star to us.

"It's cool. My grandpa and I have this new connection now," he says.

I feel a little silly that I thought he was going to kiss me.

"Plus, it really helps me get out my anger," he says. "So it's good for a lot of things."

"That's true. I guess it's always better to get out your feelings. In whatever way you can," I say. "Claire taught me that."

"Yeah," he says. "I have a long way to go before I get to Claire's level of letting things out. She says whatever pops into her head. But I'm getting there."

I nod and offer a reassuring smile.

"I'll walk you home," he says. "Okay?"

"Okay," I say. My stomach rumbles, despite the ice cream we just ate.

"What are you having for dinner?" he asks. "Hopefully

Frederick's Fish reopens soon. I know you love it there."

"I'm not sure what we're having, actually."

Calvin tells me how his mom always has a meal schedule. Mondays they have pasta, Tuesdays they have salmon, Wednesdays they have stir-fry, and so on.

I listen carefully, because there's something about the way Calvin tells a story. He makes whatever he's talking about sound so fun. He gives details, but not too many—just enough. And I always want to know what he's going to say next.

"So, Fridays you have chicken?" I ask.

And then he stops walking. So I stop walking, too. I'm not sure why he stops.

I ask, "Chicken on the bone? Or chicken cutlets?"

He doesn't answer.

He kisses me instead.

He kisses me right there in front of the farm stand that hasn't reopened yet. He kisses me right on the lips.

He pulls back from the kiss. "Chicken cutlets. With onions."

I cover my mouth, laughing and laughing. Part nervous laugh, part real laugh. Laughing because we just kissed, my first real kiss, and he's still talking about Friday-night chicken.

"Phew," he says. "I've been thinking about doing that for a long time. I'm glad it's done."

"Do you mean you're glad it's over?" I ask, embarrassed.

With lowered eyes, he says, "No. I was just nervous about it. I'm glad I got up the courage."

"Me too."

When we get to my house, he tells me to have a good dinner, and he says, "So, I'll see you tomorrow?"

"Yup."

I wonder if I should tell Micayla, or anyone, or if I even want to. But I push all of that away for now. I like that it's a secret only the two of us know.

It turns out that the impromptu Centennial Summer celebration needs to be really impromptu. Like, tomorrow.

Josh's mom and aunts are coming with the buyer in two days. Something about proving to them that the building was able to withstand the storm, and something else having to do with taxes and deadlines and all this stuff I don't understand.

Mrs. Pursuit tells me that we can't get any carnival rides, because even though they're from an off-island place, many of them were damaged in the storm.

"We'll just make do with what we have," Mrs. Pursuit says, and I can't tell if she's saying that for me or for herself. It looks like she's walking around with a cloud of disappointment over her head. But I don't feel that way. Not at all.

After your first kiss, you walk around with the sun shining

down on you, day and night. You stop at every mirror to see if you look different, to see if anything about you has changed. I can't really see the difference, but I feel that there's a little bit of ballet in every step I take.

"I'll put up these posters, and you hand out these fliers and tell everyone to show up around noon. And I'll go around to whatever restaurants are open and ask them to bring food. It'll be great," Mrs. Pursuit says with a sigh. "Okay?"

"We don't have to do this, you know," I tell her. "Maybe Seagate isn't ready for it yet."

Somehow I feel that she's doing this for me. Maybe only for me. To cheer me up.

"No, we *need* to," she says. "We need to boost the spirits on the island. Plus, like you said a long time ago, one hundred years is a big deal."

"I said that?" I ask her.

She hands me the stack of fliers. "Yes. And you were right."

I convince the others to come help me hand them out. It feels a little funny to be with Calvin and the rest of the group. We have this secret that nobody else knows. And every few minutes, our eyes will meet, and we'll grin.

When we're done passing out the fliers, we set up chairs in the hotel lobby and make sure the stage area has a working microphone and outlets nearby. The vendors will set up outside.

"They're really selling this place?" Bennett asks me.

I shrug. "That's what Josh said."

"But it's the only hotel on Seagate. It won't be the same if it becomes part of some big chain," Micayla says. "There are a few bed-and-breakfasts, but not many. Where will all the guests stay for my wedding? I need a place with character."

"You're getting married?" I giggle. "You didn't tell us!"

She plops down on one of the chairs. "You know what I mean. Eventually."

"Well, this will still be a hotel," I say. "Maybe it won't be that bad. And who knows? Maybe Josh can buy it back one day. When he's older, when either his acting or his veterinary career takes off."

"I guess," she groans.

"Who's getting married?" Bennett asks, making it clear he was eavesdropping as he set up chairs.

"Micayla," I say.

"I'll be a bridesmaid," he says.

I giggle. "Huh? You mean a groomsman."

"No, at my cousin Lola's wedding, she had a male brides-maid, her best friend since first grade," he explains. "Everyone thought it was cool. I thought it was cool, too."

"I can't wait for my wedding," Micayla says. "There will be flowers everywhere . . ."

As Micayla goes on and on, I see Calvin in the back of the room, finishing a row of chairs. I turn around to get a glimpse of him.

And it makes me wish I could peek into the future right

now. For one tiny second, I'd like to pull the curtain back to reveal my wedding day. I want to see who the groom is and what I'm wearing and if Micayla is my maid of honor. But then I close the imaginary curtain and put the idea out of my mind.

Instead I think about Calvin. And my first kiss. And how much I like him. And how proud I am that he's such a caring person.

And I also think about Bennett. I'm so lucky to have a best friend who's both a boy *and* willing to be a bridesmaid at a wedding.

I don't care about pulling the curtain open again, because right now feels pretty good.

44

"*Welcome, everyone,*" *Mrs. Pursuit says. There* are only about thirty people there. "We couldn't let Seagate's centennial summer pass without some kind of celebration. It's been a rough season, and we've faced some tough times, but we're still here." She laughs. "We're Seagaters. We're resilient. So, sit back and enjoy the show."

Most of the people who signed up to perform are back on the island. And they take the stage, one by one, entertaining people, making everyone smile. It's not the same as we imagined it, with a view of the ocean and carnival rides, but it's something. And we're happy to have it.

The father-son juggling duo wows the crowd.

Josh and the Improvimaniacs are funnier than ever. Sketch after sketch, the audience laughs.

Saturday We Tennis plays our favorite summer songs.

And finally, Larry Park brings his keyboard up to the stage, and my skin prickles. I'm suddenly sad that Lester isn't here to listen to the finale at our birthday party for Seagate.

Larry is halfway through his Bach Invention when we hear it.

Barking! Excited, high-pitched barking.

Lester! He's here! And he's singing along!

Lester runs up to the front of the room, tilts his head back, and sings in his half-singing, half-howling way. And everyone loves it. The crowd cheers and claps. And Larry Park is happy to have his singer back.

At the end of the performances, after an extra-long dance party with Saturday We Tennis, Mr. Brookfield surprises everyone. Including me.

He walks right up onto the stage. Calvin goes with him.

"What kind of Seagate celebration would it be without the Scream?" he says.

And together, they scream.

"AAAAHEEEEOOWWWWW!"

People love it and give the famous scream an instant standing ovation.

A feeling of pride washes over me again.

"Did you know he was going to do that?" I whisper to Claire.

"Nope." She shakes her head. "Come with me. There's something we need to do."

We run up onto the stage, and then Claire takes a big breath and screams *"Aaaaheeeeoowwwww!"* and she motions for me to do it, too. So I try. *"Aaaaheeeeoowwwww!"* And then we scream together. *"AAAAHEEEEOOWWWWW!"*

Everyone stays standing and cheering and clapping.

All the stress, sadness, frustration, and worry of our stormy summer pours out of us through the scream. We release it. And it feels so good.

"That was awesome," I whisper as we walk off the stage. "How are you doing? I know you hate when I ask if you're okay. So I'm asking this way instead. How are you?"

"I'm okay," she says. "Really."

I reach over and hug her, and she smiles.

A few minutes later, as everyone is milling about, eating and chatting, I go to find Lester and his family.

"I didn't know you guys came back," I say.

"We wanted to surprise you," Lester's owner-mom says. "We never really knew how much Lester missed singing to classical music on the piano until the day you found him before the storm. Now we play classical music for him all the time, and guess what: he doesn't try to run away anymore. He seems so happy now. Thank you for helping us, Remy. Lester is back to his old self, thanks to you!"

It makes me so happy that I've helped Lester and his family.

"He was born to sing!" I say.

And then I realize that Lester wasn't really running away *from* anything. Lester was running *toward* something, something good, something he loved. I can relate.

I'm so happy to be back on Seagate.

45

After the celebration, my friends and I walk to Sundae Best.

"Surprise Scoops for everyone?" I ask them.

"Sounds good," Claire says. "I was getting pretty tired of raspberry cream."

We sit and eat our ice cream. Some people are pleased with their Surprise Scoops and some aren't, so we pass our bowls around the table so we can sample them all and trade for flavors people like better.

Josie laughs at our commentary on the flavors. "Okay, okay, I get it. No one's into the sweet-potato ice cream. Noted."

"We tried it," I offer.

"That's all I ask." She shrugs. "It's like the sign says." She points to a beachy-looking sign behind the counter: BE OPEN TO SURPRISES.

We finish our ice cream, and Calvin, Bennett, Claire, and Micayla decide to walk to the Seagate community pool. It's open for swimming, and it's sunny out, and everyone wants to jump in. Claire's worrying about her tan again, just like old times, and I'm grateful for that.

I tell them I'm going to take Marilyn Monroe home, and I'll meet them there. On the walk home, I think about what Josie said when she came back after the storm—how God loves ice cream. I guess that's true. The store was completely spared.

I think about her signs: ICE CREAM IS MY RELIGION and BE OPEN TO SURPRISES.

Josie believes in Surprise Scoops, and now I do, too. Every day is pretty much a Surprise Scoop, I guess.

Some scoops you like, others you don't. Sometimes you want to have the same scoop every day, and some days you have to be pushed to try a new one, because you're afraid of how it will taste.

Like the time I got that key-lime-pie scoop. I hated it. I pushed it to the side and ate my chocolate-milk-and-cookies scoop as fast as I could so the key lime wouldn't melt into it and turn it all sour. But the strange thing was that the key lime pie actually made the chocolate and cookies taste even better.

I think I have a new sign idea for Josie. I'll have to tell her the next time I see her. And I can't wait to share it with my friends, because I know they'll understand:

LIFE IS ONE BIG SURPRISE SCOOP.

ACKNOWLEDGMENTS

Thanks to Tamar Brazis and everyone at Amulet for all of their hard work on this book.

So much love and gratitude for Dave, Aleah, and Hazel. You bring sunshine on the cloudiest of days.

Many thanks to the Greenwalds and Rosenbergs for all of their support.

ABOUT THE AUTHOR

Lisa Greenwald is the author of *Welcome to Dog Beach*, *Reel Life Starring Us*, *Sweet Treats & Secret Crushes*, and the Pink & Green series. She works in the library at the Birch Wathen Lenox School in Manhattan. She is a graduate of The New School's MFA program in writing for children and lives in Brooklyn. Visit her online at lisagreenwald.com.

Check out a sample chapter from Lisa Greenwald's

bestselling Pink & Green series!

My Life in
Pink & Green

LISA GREENWALD

Beauty tip: Putting cold cucumbers on your eyes can reduce puffiness and relieve stress.

Things can always be worse. That's what Grandma says, anyway, whenever something really bad happens. I've always thought that was a pretty good way to look at life. But lately I'm not so sure, because I don't think things can really get any worse.

It's Friday afternoon—a time when most normal seventh-grade girls would be at a friend's house or maybe the mall or even the movies.

But where am I?

The pharmacy.

And what am I doing?

Opening mail.

When I'm at the pharmacy after school, it's my job to open the mail. I do it first thing so that I have the rest of the time free. But it's not like there's so much for me to do the rest of the time. It's not like if I don't open the mail first thing, I won't have time to do it later. I just don't like to have things hanging over my head.

I bet most kids my age would find opening the mail to be the most boring thing in the world. And sometimes it is. But it's also kind of comforting. I like coming to the pharmacy straight from school and having my snack in the back office.

It's nice to know you always have a place to go.

Besides, I don't usually read the mail; I just open it and put it in a neat pile. But today big, bold, black letters catch my eye: THREE DELINQUENT MORTGAGE PAYMENTS. My throat starts to feel like it's getting tighter and tighter, almost like it's closing up. And my heart starts beating fast and furious, when it was beating calmly just a second ago.

THREE DELINQUENT MORTGAGE PAYMENTS. What does that mean? That we haven't paid the mortgage for three months? Or that the payments weren't enough?

The next sentence: YOU ARE IN DANGER OF FORECLOSURE.

We get a lot of mail at the pharmacy because we get all of the business mail, obviously, and all of our regular mail too. The pharmacy is like our second home. Lately I'm beginning to think we spend more time there than at our real house.

"Jane!" Grandma calls. I see her coming into the office, and I try to put the letter under the stack of regular mail, but I'm not quick enough. Grandma hasn't even said hi to me yet and already she's upset. "Jane Scarlett Desberg!"

Even though my mom's forty, my grandma still uses her whole name when she's angry at her.

"Ma, what?" My mom comes into the office, her cleaning apron only half on. She was in the middle of dusting and reorganizing her favorite section of the store—the magazine area. Old Mill Pharmacy doesn't just carry the usual magazines like *People* and *Glamour* and *Time*. We have those, but we also carry magazines that are hard to find on the average drugstore news rack, like the *Nation* and the *Progressive*.

My mom's a huge reader. She'll read anything she can get her hands on, and especially stuff about people making a difference or taking a stand on complicated issues. She doesn't just accept situations as they are—she's always questioning things, so she likes to read magazines and newspapers that reflect that state of mind.

She's one of those people who truly believe one person can change the world.

"'Three delinquent mortgage payments'—that's what!" Grandma shoves the letter in front of my mom's nose. "'In danger of foreclosure'! Can you please explain?"

My mom rolls her eyes and fastens her apron around her waist, admiring herself in the office's full-length mirror. "Oh, Ma. They always say that. We'll pay. Don't worry. I've been putting off our last few payments to save up for the Small Businesses, Big World conference I told you about. We need to do more than just fill prescriptions. Our business can make a difference in the world. We just need to find out what we can do."

Grandma's face falls. The tension in the room seems to be expanding like a balloon that's about to pop. This is my time to walk away. "I'm going to straighten up the toy section!" I say, more cheerfully than I'd normally say it.

But instead of straightening, I close the door and wait outside the office so that I can eavesdrop. I need to find out what *foreclosure* means.

I make fake walking sounds so that Mom and Grandma think I'm far enough away that I won't be able to hear them, and then I scooch down toward the floor and gently press my ear against the wooden door.

"Jane, time to come out of your save-the-world daze, sweetheart," Grandma says. "We don't have enough money to save the world. We need to save this pharmacy. You have two children to support. And frankly, I'm sick of having to tell you this."

"Ma, relax," Mom says, acting like she has everything under control. There's a long silence, and I'm wondering if the conversation's over and if I really should go and clean the toy section.

"We're sitting down tonight with all of the bills," Grandma says, sounding calmer now. "And I'm letting Tory and Charise go. I have to. I don't have a choice."

Tory and Charise have been working at the pharmacy for as long as I can remember. Tory does all of the loading and unloading of boxes and stocking of the shelves. And Charise makes sure the pharmacy's spick-and-span and helps out behind the counter. She always tells me stories about the old days, when people would have to wait in line for sodas and snacks and stuff. I even remember when Grandpa was alive and so many of the kids in our neighborhood would hang out at the store, having snacks at the counter after school. Sometimes Grandpa would even help them with their homework.

It's not like that anymore. Not at all.

Nowadays, people will occasionally come in for a soda, but they're usually high school kids who are going to the movies next door and don't want to pay movie-theater prices. No one ever orders items from the grill; Grandma barely even turns it on anymore. Things have changed a lot, and not in a good way. I wish there was a way to go back to the way they used to be.

I especially feel bad for Tory and Charise. I know they need the money. And I know Grandma would never let them go if she didn't have to.

That's how I know things are bad.

Check out these other great reads by
Lisa Greenwald!

My Summer of
Pink & Green

LISA GREENWALD

THE THIRD BOOK IN THE *PINK & GREEN* SERIES

Pink & Green
IS THE
NEW BLACK

LISA GREENWALD

LISA GREENWALD

Reel Life
STARRING US